**EyeCue Productions
Presents**

CHUMP

DUNCAN P. BRADSHAW

Chump First Published in 2016

Published by EyeCue Productions

Cover and internal illustrations by Jon Dixon

http://www.dixondoesdoodles.com/

Cover and internal design by EyeCue Productions

ISBN 978-0993534638

ACKNOWLEDGEMENTS

Shout out to Thomas S. Flowers III, for bugging me about making a zombie western, though it's not a full length book, I hope you enjoy it.

Adrian Shotbolt, for the inspiration for another story, just a little thank you for your continued support.

Likewise Daryl Duncan, rarely do you meet someone in life that surpasses expectation, a true legend.

Adam Millard for proofreading this and getting it all spick and span. I swear to all that is unholy that I will take on board the corrections.
This time.

Zombie Ed, if it wasn't for you inviting me back to the Festival of Zombie Culture in 2016, most of these stories wouldn't even exist, cheers dude.

Debbie, for reading my barely formed drivel and laughing out loud, usually in the right places. I always get a good sense of what works and what doesn't, just from your facial expressions, thank you. Plus, you came up with a half-decent title huh?

DEDICATION

You.
Yes, you.
Thank you.

CONTENTS

chump

Pronunciation: /tʃʌmp/

NOUN

1 *informal* A foolish or easily deceived person.

2 *British* The thick end of something, especially a loin of lamb, mutton or human flesh.

MILLIE

DUNCAN P. BRADSHAW

MILLIE

Young Millie was a prepper,
Her bug out bag always packed,
From tents and knives to pots and pans,
Her cupboards were always stacked.

Not a day went by when she stopped to count,
If she had enough cans of beans,
Boxes of matches, bags and toilet roll,
Bottled water from Celtic springs.

She'd stop and speak to one and all,
Whoever would dare to listen,
About the simple truth,
Her raison d'être, motto, and mission;

"To properly prepare for the apocalypse,
One first must make a list,
You never know when it will finally start,
What could be the catalyst?
Maybe you'll find yourself in church,
Perhaps soaking in the tub?
Some are bound to be asleep,
Others pissed up in the pub."

Unfortunately for our Millie,
The day she longed to see,
Came during the daily nine to five,
At approximately ten to three.

"I work in advertising," she told her folks,
Maybe this went a tad too far,
She'd spend her day holding a cardboard sign,
Pimping cocktails for a bar.

You might not think this very strange,
Or actually really care,
But the uniform she wore for this task,
Meant she dressed up as a bear.

She didn't get to fulfil her wish,
As when the undead came,
They caught her easily in their grip,
The padded suit to blame.

Poor Millie died and lay face down,
As shoppers were torn apart,
Eventually she stood back up,
Utterly famished, and made a start.

She stalked the shops and bashed at doors,
Looking for fresh meat,
And when she got her paws on them,
She'd start off with their feet.

So should you chance upon the mall,
One thing you'll find a hoot,
Is that one young lady lurking inside,
Still wearing that bear suit.

The moral of this story is,
That if you ever get bit,
What you're wearing will be forever,
So don't dress like a tit.

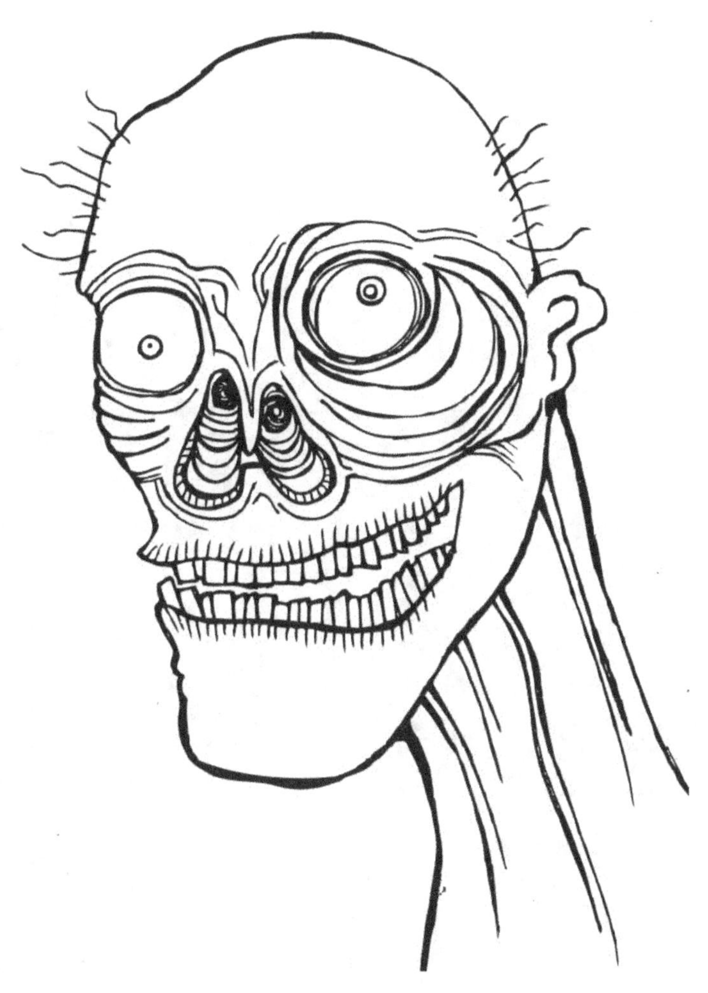

CURE WHAT AILS YA

"Step right up, ladies and gentlemen. I am here today, in this fine town of yours, to offer you the chance to purchase a bottle of my Flowers Powers liniment. Named after yours truly, Thomas S. Flowers, the third.

"I, good folk of Lobo, come here with my patented miracle potion. It cures impetigo, loosening of the bowels, curling toenails, consumption, lack of vim and vigour, and, for the ladies of this fair town, it invigorates parts of the man that other tonics just cannot reach," Thomas began his, by now, well-honed sales pitch.

The crowd, numbering around twenty, looked from one to another, shielding their eyes from the noon sun bearing down on them. Cletus turned to his wife Mary. "Does this idiot not know who runs this town? If the Martins catch him, he's gonna end up like the others."

Mary shrugged. In truth, she was more fascinated by the salesman's bona fide promise to put the lead back in her husband's pencil. It had been two and a half years since he was last able to fulfil his matrimonial duties.

Sure, she knew as well as anyone that the promises of a stranger, with a cart laden down with bottles of cloudy liquid, were as reliable as an ornery coyote doing her washing. But still…perhaps it would be worth getting a small bottle, just to see if she could coax some life back into Cletus' trouser snake.

"Why, I rode in to see you wonderful folk, having spent the last week in the town of Valentine—"

The mere mention of the neighbouring town brought out a chorus of theatrical booing and caterwauling. Thomas raised his hands to try to quell the noise.

They're gonna be eating outta the palm of my hand in no time.

"Hey now, I know what you're thinking, and…you're right. I spent a week in that town, if you could call that den of inequity a civilised place, and I have to say that not one of them seemed to appreciate what I was offering them. On the first day, a man came up to me, and it was evidently apparent to everyone that he was afflicted with the leprosy."

A number of the crowd dry-wretched; some of the more well-to-do citizens fanned themselves. "Dirty bastards," shouted Old Sweary Ned, famed for being old and potty-mouthed, hence his wholly appropriate name.

"Settle down now. That man could not help being afflicted by this hideous disease. I told him, straight out, there and then, that Flowers Powers would not only rid him of his terrible burden, but it would also help to grow back the fingers he had lost through accident or intention.

"Now, ladies and gentlemen, I know that you intelligent folk have seen enough charlatans enter your town, making promises that they couldn't keep, but I can assure you that I am a man of my word. I offered to prove to this poor man that my liniment would cure what ails him. Do you know what he did?"

A few people mumbled noncommittally.

"I said. DO YOU KNOW WHAT HE DID?"

This galvanised the audience, who replied with huge shouts of, "NO," and other such responses. Old Sweary Ned uttered an expletive-laden sentence, which cannot be printed, lest it cause offence.

Bring 'em home Tommy.

"He spat on my boots and called me a liar. Now folks, I don't mind telling you this for nothing, for I bear no shame of what I thought. I said to myself, hey mister, you deserve to suffer unbearably until your inevitable end.

"Here's what I'm gonna do for you fine people of Lobo. I'm gonna offer one of you the same deal as I offered that repugnant man. Tell me, is there one among you who is afflicted terribly?"

The crowd, which was growing steadily in number, looked from one to another, discussing their ailments and assorted infections. After a few moments, hands began to punch the air. People begged to be cured; they jostled, bustled, hustled, and other adjectives ending in –tled. Thomas surveyed the crowd, looking for the one.

"You sir." He pointed to a hand which had a red handkerchief tied around its wrist.

"Me?" the man asked.

"Yessir, you there. Come on up now, don't be shy."

People tutted and lowered their hands, craning their neck to see the one who had been selected. Eventually, the man made his way to the front of the audience, where Thomas had pulled out another upturned wooden box and placed it next to his own. "Take a perch right here, young fella. Let me get a good look at ya." Cautiously, the man stepped up onto the crate and lifted his arms, allowing Thomas to pat him down. "My, my, what an unfortunate state of disrepair I find you in today. Tell me sir, do you suffer from a shortness of breath?"

The man nodded.

"I thought so. And when you wander the dusty plains in the morning, do you cough and splutter?"

The man nodded.

"Ah-ha, we're getting closer. At night, when the sun disappears over the horizon, do you find yourself plagued with thoughts of malevolence towards your fellow man?"

The man paused, then nodded, before looking down at the floor, perhaps hoping it would swallow him whole. Some of the townsfolk shared nervous glances, hands fell onto holstered pistols.

"I knew it! You, sir, suffer from what us doctors call, *Fearsome Terror Syndrome*. It is a common disease among single men, yet to marry and father a child. Tell me, son, these folk here are as sharp as a tack, they're gonna want to see something real that I can cure. Do you have any visible injuries? Say, as a result of your need to fight in bare knuckle bouts in the corrals, outta town?"

With a look of shock, the man nodded gently before pulling up his shirt to reveal a purple welt on his ribs. A small length of bone protruded from the wound. One woman in the audience gasped and fainted. Thomas held out his hands, "Don't you fret, ladies and gentlemen. Watch as I apply Flowers Powers to this man's broken ribs, and repair the damage done by his mighty mean brain disease."

Pulling a cloth from his waistcoat pocket, Thomas poured a healthy slug of the tonic into the handkerchief and approached the man. "Now, this may sting a little. I want you to think of the lord, and pray to him for strength. Can you do that for me?"

The man nodded.

Thomas turned to his congregation, now in thrall to his every word. "Ladies and gentlemen of Lobo, I ask you to also pray to the almighty. Give this man courage, and make him not bend his knee to the devil of pain."

With one hand on the patient's shoulder, Thomas thrust the sodden cloth against the man's ribs, causing him to wince. As if he were polishing a doorknob, Thomas twisted his hand, rubbing the tonic over the affected area. After wiping a bead of sweat from his head, he yanked his hand free and shouted, "Hallelujah! He is cured!"

The entire audience strained to look at the man on top of the box, who was patting his torso down. "I don't…I don't believe it." He held his shirt up and revealed a clean patch of skin. No bruise. No sticking out piece of bone, nothing.

The woman, who had fainted previously, regained her senses, saw the after-effects, gasped once more, and collapsed to the floor. "It's a miracle!" someone in the audience exclaimed.

Chad Clark, owner of the general store and witness to many acts of rampant bullshit, shook his head. As he went to head back to his shop, the sound of hooves thudding against the bone dry floor stopped him in his tracks. "Oh no…it's the Martins," he muttered to himself.

It must've been a common saying, as the sentence was repeated in mumblings throughout the gathering. A group of five men, all wearing black and sporting glistening silver pistols, rifles and shotguns, made their way through the crowd, which parted like someone had just dropped a real bad eggy one.

The lead hombre, a mean looking SOB replete with handlebar moustache and greying beard, chewed on a cigar as his horse bumped a small family of three out of the way to get to the front.

Thomas could feel his jaw falling; his sphincter opened and closed as if it were chewing on a tough piece of armadillo steak. He clicked back into his spiel. "Why, good day to you, sir, and your four trusty amigos. Don't feel too bad about missing my demonstration, for I'd be happy to offer you and your kin a substantial discount."

With the crowd parted and silenced, the head honcho took a last pull on his cigar before stubbing it out into his leather glove covered hand. "You're new to these parts, aintcha?"

Thomas could feel his guts gurgling, and hoped it wasn't audible. "Why, yes I am, sir. I am Thomas S. Flowers. The third. From Houston. And ever since I discovered my miracle concoction, I've been selling it to all and sundry in the Lone Star State. The finest state in the United States of America."

"That it is, boy. Well, these are my brothers. Don't ask why we don't look the same, as we have diff'rent fathers. My name is Jeffery Xavier Martin. But, everyone calls me X, isn't that right?" X turned around and addressed the gathering, who nodded emphatically in agreement.

"Pleasure to meet you, Mister X." Thomas offered a hand.

"It's just X. Don't *Mister* me boy."

"Oh…okay, I'm sorry. *X*,"

"Say, I caught the end of your act. Would you mind coming here for a moment?"

Thomas could feel the call of his horse and cart, willing him to get back on the stoop and get the fuck out of Lobo, but he knew he would barely be able to turn around before he was shot. "Sure thing, X."

Standing by his side, Thomas looked up into the steely eyes of X, who lit another cigar and puffed smoke hoops into the salesman's face. "Say now, boy, why don't you give me that handkerchief of yours."

Now, Thomas was sure that he had just gulped. A plain autonomic response to a variety of things. However, in the confines of his skull, it sounded like someone had just fired a cannon at a dam, right next to his head. "My handkerchief? But…but…there's nothing in there you need to see, sir."

X smiled, though it was as warm and welcoming as taking a shit in a nest of vipers, with a dead mouse hanging from the end of the old tallywacker. "Now, boy, up until now I've been real nice to you. You can either give me the handkerchief, or I can get my brother Earl here to shoot you in the shoulder with his shotgun, and pick it up from your raggedy-ass hand lying on the dirt. Choose. But make it quick, as Earl so loves shooting folk in the shoulder."

Grudgingly, Thomas held his hand out. X took the handkerchief and opened it up. A smile birthed on his face. Throwing the stained hankie onto the floor, he held up the piece of bone which had previously been sticking out of the patient's chest. The audience gasped in shock. "Well, well, well, looks like someone here has been trying to pull the wool over people's eyes."

"I can explain, you see—"

Before he could complete his explanation, X's hand reached down, scooped out his Smith and Wesson, and with lightning speed, cracked a shot off, which caught the tonic volunteer square in the throat.

A fountain of blood jetted from the wound, and the miraculously healed man collapsed to the dusty street, gurgling on his own fluids. Thomas turned to the man. "Travis! Oh man…"

X threw the bone at the back of Thomas' head. "Hey now, boy, why don't you use your snake oil on him? Won't it save him? Patch up the nasty nick and make him all better?"

Tearing himself from the blood-soaked body of Travis, who was trying and failing to plug the wound with his fingers, Thomas said, "Please, sir…I implore you, let me be on my way. I get the picture. I won't bother you or this town no more."

Travis slapped the ground with his free hand and coughed up a wad of blood; a large blood bubble ballooned from his mouth. With a POP, it burst. His chest deflated and he leaked the relevant fluids from every bodily orifice.

X pulled the hammer back on his pistol. "Of course, of course. Tell you what. I am nothing if not a fair man. So I'm gonna count to twenty, and in that time you have to get on your horse and get out of this town. If you make it to the Blacksmiths down over yonder, then you're a free man. Deal?"

Thomas wiped a sleeve across his brow. "Of course, sir, thank ya, thank ya."

He'd taken just one step towards his horse when a voice boomed from behind him, "Twenty."

Turning, Thomas stuttered, "But…what happened to the other numbers?"

X raised his gun. "My mama was too busy getting pregnant than teaching me how to count." With that, and a wicked smile, he loosed off the remaining five bullets into Thomas' torso, each impact making him twitch like a poorly controlled puppet.

As a pall of smoke trickled out of the barrel, Thomas fell to the floor. A puddle of blood oozed out beneath him, making a claggy paste as it mixed with the dust. "Take him and that other dumb fuck out to the pit, Billy-Bob."

Billy-Bob, the youngest of the Martin clan—with six toes on his right foot and a cleft lip—nodded and climbed off his horse. "While you're there, Billy-Bob, dump all that snake oil in the pit too. We don't want anyone else getting hold of that stuff, trying to hoodwink these good folk now, huh?"

"No, X, we sure don't. I'll get on it right away," Billy-Bob lisped. He picked Thomas' body up under the armpits and dragged him to the back of the cart.

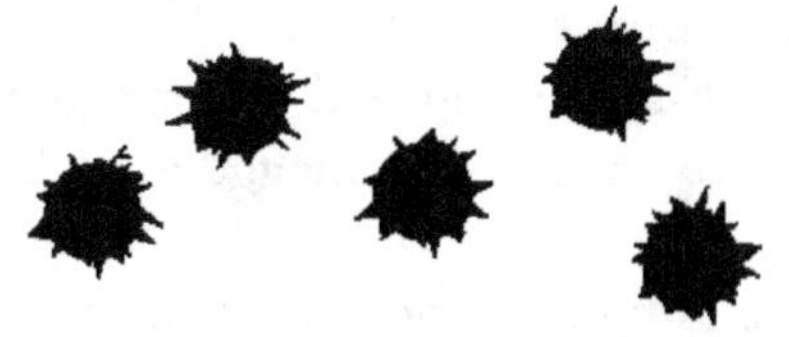

True to its moniker, the pit was a ten-foot-square ditch, dug by an errant chain-gang of Chinese railroad workers. Anyone foolish enough to incur the wrath of the Martin brothers found themselves filled with lead and flung into its dusty depths. It was much like a desert trifle, instead of layered fruit, jelly, custard and lady fingers, this one consisted solely of tiers of dead bodies covered with lime.

The base layer was made up of the rotting Chinese workers who, having abandoned the railroad construction one night, fell foul of the Martins the next day. Shortly after having excavated their own grave, and that of the future incumbents, they were the first people to feel its earthy embrace and al fresco aspect.

Since then it had been added to with a multitude of miscreants, bounty hunters, slack-jawed yokels, back-talking prostitutes, prospectors and law officials. Even a small group of Jehovah's Witnesses—who had made the mistake of interrupting X when he was breaking in his new spittoon—were interred within.

Billy-Bob grabbed hold of Thomas' foot and yanked him from the back of the cart. Landing with a puff of dust and a solid thud, Billy-Bob hawked up a thick wad of brown spit and gobbed on the dead man's face. With a punky sneer brought on by his facial malady, the hoodlum dragged the salesman's body to the edge of the pit and peered into the burrow.

"Ha, there you are, padre. I told you I'd be back, din't I? My brother told me that what you did to me was wrong. There's no kinda snake that has no eyes and cries thick milky tears. Shoulda known when it tasted different than my ma's tittie milk," Billy-Bob drawled. Father Darrin stared vacantly back, mouth agape. Necrotic hands reached upwards, coated in a fine film of lime.

With his boot on the corpse's back, Billy-Bob pushed Thomas into his new accommodation before adding more spit, seemingly the mortar in this particular trifle.

After throwing Travis' body into the ditch, he checked his horse for the bag of lime. "Dagnabbit, I gone left it in the barn. I'll have to come back tomorrow. Shoot. An' I was hopin' that I'd be able to get some more cattle rustlin' done in tha mornin'."

Retreating back to the cart, Billy-Bob picked up the wooden crate of tonic and tottered to the edge of the pit. Along the way, he put to use his recent attempts at learning to read the written word, "Ma…to…ni…Flow…damn, I can't read this non-sense," he muttered, before giving up and sticking to what he was good at. He gobbed into the pit once more, unwittingly hitting the holy man, bull's eye, in his open mouth.

Pulling the bottle stopper out with his teeth, Billy-Bob took a whiff of the oily liquid within. "Mmm, smells like Timmy-Tim when he done gone taken a pee after eating corn for two weeks. With maybe a hint of burnt cactus."

After a quick check behind him, he dabbed a little of the liniment on a nagging sore, which had been driving him potty since he'd snagged the larger of his three testicles on his aging saddle.

After enjoying the strange tingling sensation in his undercrackers, he smiled, and began to pour the liquid into the pit. As it hit the lime, it hissed, sending up wraiths of smoke, which smelt of bad guts and overflowing latrines.

Placing a hand over his mouth, he lobbed the bottle into the darkness. The smell threatening to bring up his dinner of dried root soup and lightly fried tumbleweed croutons. He set the crate down.

Using the hilt of his pistol, he smashed the top from each of the bottles. With each one now topless, he pulled his neck cloth over his nose and slung the crate into the void below.

Hearing it hit the decomposing bodies within, he nodded, and repeated the process with the other crates.

The smell still burning the back of his throat, he climbed back on the horse and cart and set out for the Martin homestead, identifiable from distance by the burning crosses.

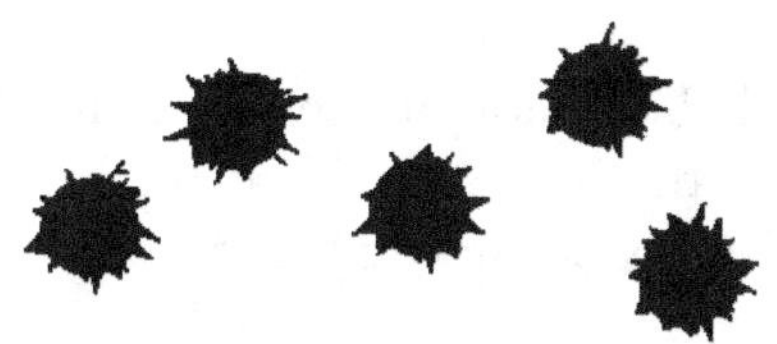

On the outskirts of Lobo, the Livreamours kept themselves to themselves, with a small farm specialising in ducks and geese. Considered niche farmers, they ground out a living selling their wares to the upper echelons of Texan society.

Whilst Greg rocked on his favourite rocking chair on the porch, Shelley checked on the animals for the final time of the night, making sure that none had fallen foul of the wolves which Lobo was infamous for.

Greg pulled a cloth out from his dungarees, and slowly buffed his rifle barrel up to a gleaming sheen. "Say, Shelley, sure is a pretty night tonight, huh?"

Trying desperately to get her evening chores done, so that she could retire to bed with her dog-eared copy of *Wuthering Heights*, she sighed. "Yes, it's mighty purty." The subtext was that she would be able to start reading a lot quicker if Greg got off his backside and quit polishing that damn rifle of his. Chiding herself for her thoughts, she finished up counting the ducks. After seeing that they were all present and correct, and lined up nicely in a row, she closed their house up for the night.

Shutting the gate behind her, Shelley dusted her hands together. Poultry farming sure was hard work, but it had a certain charm and appeal that cattle farming lacked. Feeling content with another day done, she began to pull the pins from her hair and made her way back to the farmhouse.

A bank of mist and fog rolled from the horizon. She stopped and stared at it, trying to work out if it was caused by a pack of tornado wolves, the creatures which her papa used to tell her tales of. They'd spin out of the night, in a great whirlwind, and anyone or anything caught in its wake would be swept away, never to be seen again. Though the tornado wolves stories often came after her papa had been at the moonshine, she was always wary.

Borne aloft on the breeze, above the shoulder-high wall of mist, came a sonorous moaning sound, as if a group of disconsolate people, near bereft of words, could manage a meagre, "Bbbbbbbaaaaahhhhh."

Shelly took a few steps towards it, confident it wasn't wind-imprisoned wolves, and craned her ear. The moaning came again, louder, more certain, and for a moment she thought it said a word. "Bbbbbrrrraaaaiiiiinnnnnssss."

She discounted this notion immediately. Who on earth would be out at this time of night, chanting that they wanted brains? Unsure, she turned to her husband, who was still caressing that damn rifle of his. "Greg! You hear that?"

"Hear what?"

"That sound on the breeze? Sounds like someone wants some brains."

"Who wants brains?"

"I don't know, do I? Sounds like a lot of them, any road. You best go and have a word with them folk, make sure they don't get any ideas in their heads about stealing our geese. You know that we get top dollar for our goose brain pâté."

Greg sighed.

Typical.

He worked hard all day long, making sure that his wife had plenty to get on with. His one earthly pleasure was to rock on his rocking chair, and make sure Bessie was cleaned up real good. He'd never actually fired Bessie. In fact, he wasn't even sure how to load it. But by golly, a man in the Wild West needed a firearm.

Nay, *had* to have a firearm.

Heck, he'd even heard rumours of some folk that had three! Knowing that unless he went to see what Shelley was on about, he wouldn't get any peace, he shouted back, "Fine, fine, I'll go take a look-see."

On creaky knees, Greg gingerly took the steps down from the porch, resting Bessie on his shoulder, like he'd seen those Mexicans do a few years back. Patting Shelley on the back, he walked towards the mist, which seemed to have come to a convenient halt a little way off, shrouding the mysterious visitors.

With an ear turned towards it, Greg held his breath, and sure as duck eggs are duck eggs, the lamentation of, "Bbbbrrraaaaiiiinnnnsss," trailed through the cool night air.

"Okay, now folks, I don't know what you're doing out here so late, but I'm gonna make things nice and clear for ya. This here is private property. We don't like folk walking around at night, saying one word, and one word only. Now, either conjugate a full sentence, or desist, and get on back to your beds. You hear me?"

The silence seemed to confirm that the interlopers had heard his words, and had decided that tonight was not the night to piss about. Just as Greg went to turn back for home, the doleful moan for brains rumbled across the prairie once more.

"For Pete's sake," Greg grumbled, turning back to the mist once more. From the murk, shapes began to materialise; one became five, became ten, twenty, then into the number ranges which made you lose count, and have to take a guess.

At the fore stumbled a man, hands held out as if reaching for a packet of chewing tobacco. Greg peered closer, then turned back to Shelley, who was picking errant feathers from her hair. "It's that dang snake oil salesman we saw go past this morning."

"What's he doing?"

"He's sorta reaching out for me…saying brains over and over again."

"Does he *want* brains, or does he *have* brains?"

"I don't think he's advertising, Shelley. Say, mister, are you asking for brains or what?"

Nothing.

"Well?"

"No answer, just more brains…say, are those bullet holes?"

"In his brains?"

"No, Shelley! In his…oh jeez…"

Just then her husband turned towards her and sprinted, something he had last done when they were courting. Thinking he would come to a halt, she stood, hands on hips, waiting for him. He bolted straight past her like an angry mallard, up the stairs and into the house.

She tutted. Her mama had warned her about men like him, but did she listen? Ah well, she would go get rid of these people herself, as per usual. "Say now, this is our land, clear off or my husband will shoot ya."

"Bbbrrrraaaiiiiinnnnnnnnssssssss."

Shelley rolled her sleeves up and stormed towards the lead figure, who walked with a lopsided gait. Greg was right. It was that good-for-nothing salesman they'd seen rumble into town earlier. Well, if it was brains he wanted…

She balled her fists. "Now look here, mister, I warned ya, and you haven't listened, so this is on *you* now." Pulling her arm back, she smacked Thomas square on the nose, breaking it, and spreading the sallow skin flat against his face. He didn't even break his stride; his next step took him to within inches of the punchy woman.

Shelley lashed out with a left hook, catching the man on the cheek. He merely rocked back upright and opened his mouth. Before Shelley could smack him again, Thomas leant in and bit her on the shoulder.

Screaming, Shelley thrashed around, trying to bat the biting salesman away, but his hold was too tight. She sank to the floor. Thomas tumbled with her. Pinning her with his knees on her arms, he shoved his cold digits into her mouth, and began to work them up the inside of her head, to the top of the skull. Shelley couldn't breathe, the hand was lodged right in her gob. She felt a tickling behind her eyes before everything went dark.

Thomas tugged on the lengths of optical nerve, pulling each eye from their socket into the centre of the skull. He crushed them in one hand and yanked them free, throwing them behind him into the night—a starter for his chums.

With his hand back inside the warmth of the woman's head, he curled jagged fingernails around her brain and scooped out fistfuls of wobbly pink ribbed tissue. After a few mouthfuls, he turned around to the rest of the horde and moaned, "Bbbbrrrrraaaiiiiinnnnnsss."

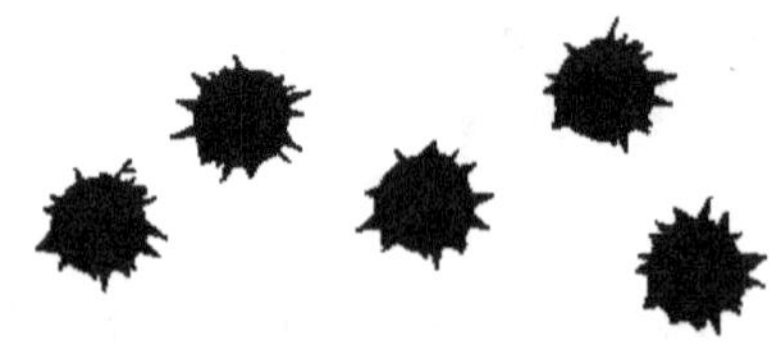

The screaming from outside ceased nearly as quickly as it had begun. Greg rested against the front door, cradling Bessie in his hands. The moaning, whilst muffled, seemed to surround him, echoing through the wooden building. He twisted his head from side to side as the wooden walls creaked and complained around him. A knocking at the front door near scared him out of his skin.

"Shelley? Is that you?" he asked, wishing there was some kind of hole bored into the wood that he could spy out of. He wasn't sure what he would call it, but it would be something snappy, like a 'miniscule viewing porthole'.

Or something.

The knocking came again. It *had* to be Shelley; she must've been struck mute or something. Whilst he considered the ramifications of that, and the wonderful bliss it would engender, he turned around and began to open the door, operating on autopilot.

Shelley was not there to greet him. Though in the few seconds afforded to him, before his jugular was severed with pegs of craggy teeth, he saw that the mouldering Jehovah's Witness chewing his throat out held a pair of crushed eyeballs in his fetid hand, which looked mighty familiar.

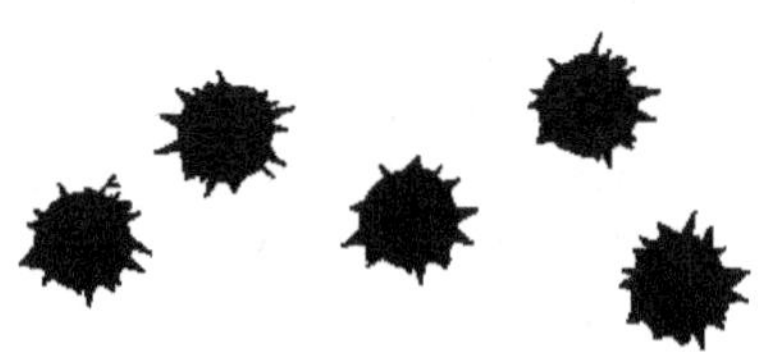

Chad barred the doors inside the General Store and began to blow out the lamps. Ruing his decision to buy in that job lot of new-fangled bear traps, which lacked the necessary spring to adequately snare any kind of mammal, he plunged his meagre takings into his cash bag and headed out back.

"Evening, Chad," Miss Elle-Louise cooed, waving coyly at him.

"Good evening, ma'am," he replied, half-distracted with locking up.

"Say, you headin' over to the saloon later?"

"Wasn't planning on it. Got a long night ahead, scraping the muck from my tin bath."

Elle-Louise chuckled to herself, then saw that he was stony faced. "Oh…you're serious. Well, if you do fancy a drink, head on over, Chad."

Double checking to make sure the premises were secure, Chad bid her farewell, before setting off in the direction of his abode. He had barely made it to the post office when he felt a cold shiver run down his spine. Pulling his jacket tighter, he looked around, peering off down the main street, out towards the edge of town.

"Huh…that's peculiar," he remarked to himself. Rolling slowly up from the pitch black plains was a swirling mist. He would have ignored it, but he saw something move within the haze. Shoving his takings into his jacket pocket—just in case these ghosts were going to try to mug him—he stumbled towards the fog, drawn to it like a ship to a whirlpool.

The hubbub of the Tex Noir bar blared behind him, an off kilter rendition of 'Where The Wild Buffalo Lays Its Hat' was being murdered by Old Sweary Ned, who substituted most of the lyrics with F-bombs. Despite the din, he swore that he could hear some kind of mantra emanating from the broiling mist.

He craned his neck, trying to make out what it was…

"Hey, Chad! How you doing?"

The words, delivered so close to his ear that it constituted as getting to first base, made Chad jump, causing the coins in his money bag to jingle. He spun around and found himself staring into the bloodshot eyes of Ian, the town drunkard.

Ian wore the same outfit every day. The only features that ever changed was the redness of his nose, depending on the amount of blood coursing through his alcohol filled veins. Not only was he a complete pisshead, he was also the dullest man in the entire state of Texas.

The folk of Lobo often commented that the imbibing of booze made even the most socially inept throw off their shackles and join in the assorted japery. It turned the shy into outgoing chatterboxes, and even those with more inhibitions than a celibate ox loosen up a little.

Ian was the exception to this rule. Some said that it was only when he was sober—which happened every couple of years—that he would become the life and soul of the party. However, in this state of sobriety, he always managed to cause some kind of town-wide scandal, which made him hit the whisky even harder than before, stripping him of his winning personality.

Allowing his skin to sink back over his skeleton, Chad could still feel his heart hammering away inside his chest, and he wondered if it would ever return to its normal tempo. "Ian…you scared me to death!"

Ian burped. It smelt of rotten crab apples and dung. "Don't get all tetchy man…you nearly stood on my dessert."

He followed the drunken man's bony finger, and saw a squashed vulture on the floor. Exposure to the baking sun and wagon wheels (the wooden kind, not modern day confectionary) had pushed the bird's innards out of its head and anus. "Don't tell me you were eating that? You can't."

"Why not? Not up to your culinary standards, Mister Fancy Dan Beef

Borgennooo…Beef Burgundy…Beef Boogaloo…Beef Borganew…you know, that French thing?"

"Running away from danger or mild peril?"

"No, you eejit. That other thing, with the beef, and the bergamot…something…"

Chad sighed, "Look Ian, as fun as this is, I've got to get home, I—"

"That's right, rub it in why don't ya? I'll just sleep under the gallows over in the town square, don't mind me!"

"Okay…I won't." Tipping his hat, Chad hurried off down the road, casting nervous glances from the moaning mist to the town lush.

Ian wobbled on unsteady feet before collapsing to the floor, where he rooted through the dried-out organs of the unfortunate vulture. With a length of intestine in his teeth and fingers, he pulled on it, trying to break the stringy twine.

Shadows staggered behind him, covering his supper in shade. "Hey…man…don't you come back here and try to steal my food."

He looked up, saw a figure with outstretched hands, a voice drawled, "Bbbbrrraiiinnnsssss."

Ian chuckled. "Nope, I had the brains first, Mister. Gotta make sure you get the best eats right off the bat, else those dang raccoons will get 'em."

Cold fingers raked his face. "Get off now, that tickles," Ian complained, before the fingernails found purchase in his nostrils. "Don't go mining in there. I gots to keep that for a palate-cleanser after, you hear me?" His words fell on deaf ears as more clammy hands ran over his skin, invading the dank folds of his greasy clothing and filthy skin.

Ian screamed as the fingers in his nostrils pushed deeper into his head, digging into his clogged up sinuses, leaking thick gloopy fluid over the intruder. Ian tried to complain, but found himself bereft of the ability to speak as another hand grabbed hold of his tongue and tugged on it forcefully.

"Bbbbbbraaaaaaaaaaaaaiiiiiiiiinnnnnnnnnnnnsssssssss," the nose-plunderer moaned, twisting his fingers around a hundred-and-eighty degrees and pulling off Ian's face in a move that would later become the inspiration for a popular nineties Hollywood film.

With the face of their dinner de-gloved, the undead mob bundled Ian. Through force of numbers, they cracked his skull open by pressing it against the baked ground. Chunks of brain squeezed through pieces of broken bone, like putty pushed through a sieve, and they fought over the slim pickings, nibbling on the chumps of meat.

"Say now, Ian, I think I mighta been a tad hasty. Why don't you come on over to mine? I think I've got some cow brains that are just sitting there…"

"Bbrrrrrrraaaaaaiiiiiiinnnnnnsssssss," Thomas echoed, having joined in the evening shambling late, after chowing down on the Livreamours.

Chad froze, he was expecting a drunkard, not a bullet-riddled snake oil salesman.

He evaded a clumsy swipe with ease, and the man fell to the floor, pawing at the dirt. "Ian? Is he with you?" Looking across to where he had left the man, he saw what remained of the town's resident alcoholic, which wasn't much.

"Holy Toledo, what is going on here?"

As if to labour the point, Thomas rose to his knees and moaned, "Bbrrraaaiinnsss," once more.

Chad began to back away as more and more of the ghouls locked eyes on him, realising that they were not going to even get sloppy seconds with the first meal sprawled out on the floor.

From the mist, people fitting the charcoal drawings of Missing and Wanted posters, staggered into view. "Aww shoot," Chad said, before turning and bolting towards the Tex Noir saloon bar at speed.

After a few cursory glances behind him, he noticed that the brains-loving cannibals were not moving particularly fast. They certainly weren't running. He made a mental note of that.

These previously dead folk sure aren't running.

Nope.

Not at all.

Not. Running.

Knowing that they weren't going to catch him up, but keen to avoid being boxed in by them, he sauntered to the bar. He didn't want to be breathless when he arrived, lest he be unable to relay this rather disturbing turn of events.

Chad pushed the batwing doors of the saloon open and, after exchanging hat tips with all and sundry, unwittingly aiding and abetting his burgeoning RSI, he made his way to the bar. "You made it!" a woman's voice exclaimed.

Turning around, he saw Elle-Louise holding the edge of her dress and skittering towards him like a can-can dancer. Chad held his hands out. "Now wait on, miss. I've got something to tell Tex first. Heck, I think the entire town might need to hear this."

"But can't we have a drink first, Chad? I'm mighty thirsty. I think I might very well faint if I don't have a double whisky with a whisky chaser," the woman said in a put-on feeble voice.

"Very well. Tex, get this woman what she wants, but tell me, is the sheriff around?"

After exuding enough saliva to refloat a beached porpoise into a whisky tumbler, Tex slung the towel over his shoulder and pulled the bottle stopper out with his teeth. He spat it onto the floor. "Nope," he replied.

"The deputy, then?"

"Nope."

"The army? Surely there must be some conscripted men around these here parts?"

"Nope."

"Well where in tarnation has the sheriff and his deputy got to? I have grave news. Grave news indeed." Seeing that the conversation was taking longer than envisaged, Chad cast a nervous glance outside. He noted that the cerebral-matter lovers were dragging their dead corpses along on unsteady legs with all they could muster.

Tex gobbed into another glass. "From what I heard, Sheriff York and his deputy are up at Van Horn, attending a three-day course on hanging bandits and advanced interrogation skills. Namely, a new method called 'Good Sheriff, Bad Sheriff'. It all sounds mighty interestin' to me. Should be back day after tomorrow, at a guess."

"Dammit…"

"Hey now, Chad. Why the long face? Say, you hear the one about the horse? Walking into the bar?"

Chad waved his hands. "Not now, Tex. There's something real strange going on in town. That fella from before? That salesman? Well he—"

A hand landed on Chad's shoulder, the force of which made his collarbone crack, and pushed him to one side. Hardly a violent man, Chad balled his fists and turned around to face the thudder. "Say now, partner, that ain't none too kind, you—"

X looked down at him; his cigar cherry bloomed as he breathed in. Chad gulped. Slowly, and intently, X removed the stub of the cigar from his mouth and dropped it onto the floor, between both men. With the toe of his boot, he extinguished it, before blowing smoke into Chad's face, making him cough.

"What was it you were saying about that salesman?"

Chad pointed to the saloon entrance. "He's out there…X…other folk with him too, some of them look mighty ripe to me. Almost like they're dead, or some such…"

Even when he laughed, X sounded like he was a freight train careening down the tracks at full speed. On fire. With its cargo of gunpowder barrels exploding. "Why of course they are, Chad. Of course they are."

"I mean it, sir. They done gone eaten up Ian."

"You mean to tell me that the lying son of a bitch who tried to hoodwink y'all earlier, the one I saved you all from by shooting him till he was dead, is outside?"

"Uh-huh."

"You're sure now, boy?"

"Uh-huh."

"So if I send Randy out there, and he don't find him, then you will have no objections to me using your lily white butt cheeks as a dartboard for the remainder of the night?"

"Well, I don't think that's fair, but I—"

X waved two fingers to the front of the bar. His brother, Randy, downed the remainder of his water—he was a devout tee-totaller, which didn't sit too well with his brothers—and moseyed on over to the swinging doors.

"Well? You see anything out there?"

Randy was stood up against the wooden doors, shaking, as if afflicted with night terrors, hands waving *a la* jazz. X turned to face the entrance. "Randy, I'm asking you a question, son. Just because we came out of mama's furry front bottom, don't mean I won't beat you senseless, boy. Now answer me. Is there anything out there?"

Still he shook, before a doleful moan came from the street outside,

"Bbbbbbbbbbbrrrrrrrraaaaaaaiiiiiiinnnnnnnnnnnsssssss."

"Brains? What the hell are you going on about, Randy?"

His body stopped shaking. Hands fell slack by his side, then his head lurched backwards, his throat chewed through. It hung briefly by a flap of skin before it tore and thudded against the dusty planks. The bar patrons went silent, except for those who were showered by arterial spray in the front few rows. They cursed and yelled, utterly miffed. Randy's body wilted to the floor, the doors creaked on the breeze.

A blue-skinned hand and arm slapped the floor around the dead body, seemingly looking for something. Its fingers felt the greasy strands of Randy's hair and pulled the head outside. There was a crunch, before an enchanting slurping sound broke up the monotony of people outside moaning about, "Bbbrrraaaiiinnnssss," once more.

X stormed across the bar. People and tables moved out of the way, either by their own volition or being hurled sideways. He wrenched the door open, and looked down to see Father Darrin with his hand plunged inside his brother's head. Like a child hollowing out a Halloween pumpkin, the man of the cloth pulled out fistfuls of brain and chomped on it.

There was a solitary gunshot as X fired at the priest, point blank in the chest. The holy man slumped to the ground, before sitting up and resuming his task. X fired again and again, fanning the hammer, unleashing round after round into his brother's despoiler. Despite being stitched from sternum to rectum, Father Darrin ignored the wounds and continued to tease strands of brain from Randy's head.

X peeked into the street, then threw himself backwards onto the floor as scores of blood-stained hands groped for him. His youngest brother, Timmy-Tim, called out, "What do you see? Did a giant lizard crawl outta the desert and shoot everyone up with eyes that lit up like the sun?"

"Nope."

"Is some kind of half-man, half-metal automaton, hell-bent on finding one particular woman to prevent some facet of the future coming to pass, about to mosey on through them doors and shoot up Tex Noir on a crazy redneck killin' rampage?"

"Nope."

"I got it! There's some kind of green-skinned aliens, with ray guns, running around, shouting ACK ACK, and vapourising all and sundry with their futuristic weaponry, all because some dumb shit released a dove of peace into the air?"

Like a crab, X scuttled backwards, slamming into the bar itself, where a conveniently placed bottle of whisky rolled off and into his hand. After taking a huge slug, he pointed to the doors. "They're coming…"

"Who's coming? Is it the Yankees again?" Timmy-Tim asked, all of his far-fetched notions exhausted.

X just shook his head. "Nope, not Yankees, mutated lizards, tin men or aliens. Looks more like the devil and his bastard demons are visiting us this night."

Picking himself up from the floor, X stood with his remaining brothers, Billy-Bob,

Timmy-Tim and Earl, all of them still reeling from the loss of Randy. Though he was as dumb as a post, he carried out important administrative matters within the Martin gang. His accountancy skills were unmatched, and he was the only brother able to lay claim to the fact that he knew, in all certainty, who his real daddy was.

*** Spoiler alert *** It was a gravedigger out of Arizona called Johnny Tucson. It has no other bearing on the story, but it might come up in a future pub quiz question.

Earl brought his shotgun to bear and cocked it, mainly because it looked and sounded cool. "What do we do now, X?"

With his senses returning, X frantically began to reload his pistols. "Get ready. As soon as those demons bust through the doors, unload on those sons of bitches. I shot the padre, must've been duff bullets, but I figure with enough of us, we should be fine."

He turned to address the bar patrons, who were all unsettled by the sound of teeth crunching on bone emanating from outside. "Y'all better get those shooting irons of yours ready. We got ourselves some uninvited guests in our fine town. Unless you want me or one of my brothers to come pay you a visit when this is all over, I suggest you open fire on anything that walks through those doors."

Silence fell. Even the slurping sounds from outside ceased. People carefully turned tables on their sides, using them as barricades, unsure of what exactly they would be facing. Others offered silent prayers or snaffled drinks from others, who were too preoccupied with other matters. Chad vaulted over the bar, seeking solace behind it, getting a raised eyebrow from Tex but nothing more.

From the entrance, above the swinging doors, came the mist, wafting in on a gentle breeze. Then the moaning began in earnest, the dead announced what they wanted from the people inside the bar. "Bbrrrraaaiinnnnsss."

Father Darrin burst through the doors, stumbling over the still-twitching feet of Randy. Stuck to his hand, necrotic fingers buried deep within the skull, he waved Randy's decapitated head. The priest's mouth was ringed with blood, as if he had been plundering jars of freshly made strawberry jam.

No sooner had he set one foot inside, than Travis was behind him. A dormouse peered out of the ragged hole in his throat, wondering what had happened to his new home. He was told by the mouse estate agent that this domicile came with stunning views, and lay on firm foundations. If he wanted a mobile home, he would've stuck to the big ol' ball of tumbleweed that he had lived in for the past year.

X yelled, "FIRE," but the pissed up people within needed no such encouragement. The wooden doorframe splintered as round after round smacked into it, the keener marksmen and women managing to at least hit the walking cadavers.

Bullets slammed into the undead, making them twitch and dance provocatively, yet did not lay them low. More and more stumbled into the breach. A few of the Chinese workers, at the back of the queue—undoubtedly the hungriest of the lot given they were the last to crawl out of their graves—pressed their faces against the windows.

The poorly made glass easily gave way, and the badly decomposed workers tumbled into the bar, body parts falling off them with ease. Landing on bemused drinkers, the Chinese stood up on disintegrating feet. Taking advantage of their surprise arrival, they grabbed hold of the nearest patrons and tucked into their first meal for eight months. Now amongst the gunfire, and monotonal assertion of the acquisition of brains, came the sound of human screaming.

"There's too many!" Billy-Bob shouted. Having already expended his bullets, he was reloading with furious abandon. "Why won't they go down?" he bellowed, having finally reloaded one pistol chamber up with fresh ammunition. He unloaded the lot into Travis, who aside from doing a wee little jig continued his inexorable march onwards.

Earl's shotgun boomed out, removing a number of the zombies' arms at the shoulders, but his weapon quickly ran dry. He began to thumb shells from his bandolier, though with trembling fingers he struggled to free them. One pinged off and landed on the floor. He dove after it, and began to scrabble amongst the empty cartridges which littered the floor, trying to find it. Father Darrin lurched forward and landed on top of him, pinning Earl to the ground.

Despite being at the wrong end, the priest wormed his fingers through the trouser seams and into the pink flesh beneath. Earl began to sing in the key of a mezzo soprano, as the interior of his groin was invaded by cold bony digits. Father Darrin pulled out a chunk of flesh and gave it a sniff, which lit his little dead eyes up. He began to shove the meat into his mouth.

Seeing this, some of his former brain-craving kin clawed out at the humans, and began to rip and tear any strip of flesh they could get their mitts on. More screaming rang out as vein, ligament, and muscle was wrenched free, and feasted upon by the horde.

The bar was now awash with the living, the dying, the dead and the newly risen dead. With guns empty, and knives doing little damage to the zombie physiology, the tide turned, and those that could, tried to flee. Unfortunately, the delay in their entrance was down to the mob surrounding Tex Noir, and any avenue of escape was now blocked by clamouring zombies, who snagged those trying to escape and brought them down.

Thomas ignored the other breathers, lumbering towards X with some filament of memory burning like a candle within. X raised his pistols and squeezed the triggers, both ending in hollow CLICKs. He dropped one to the ground and turned the other over like a makeshift club. With hands outstretched, Thomas lunged at his murderer, though X easily dodged to one side and clouted him on the side of the head as he went past. Emboldened, X watched as the salesman collapsed to the floor like a felled tree, yelling, "Thar she blows, you dumb fuck."

Amongst the blood and guts, X circled the stricken zombie. "Let's see if I can kill you again huh, *Mister*?"

Thomas, lying on his front, was trying to right himself, but failing miserably, hands unable to gain purchase on the blood-slick floor. X crouched down, one knee pushed against the small of the salesman's back. Grabbing hold of Thomas' right wrist, which was the wrong way up, X yanked it up and over like a one armed bandit machine.

There was a sickening crack as the shoulder popped out of its socket and crushed a number of smaller bones on its abrupt journey. X let the limb go and it slapped against the floor, useless. "Well I'll be damned. Looks like you ain't invincible after all, huh? Let's go see what happens when I do this…" He grabbed hold of Thomas' head, which was nose to floorboard. X twisted the head as if it were a spinning top. Thomas now looked into the eyes of the man who had killed him, though it was also a hundred and eighty degrees from where it really ought to be. "Oooooh-weee, looky here," X hollered. With some further wrenching and disentanglements, he pulled the head clean off, a two foot section of blood- and gore-covered spinal column came off with it.

Holding his trophy aloft, X slapped Thomas' face with his free hand, laughing and goading the head. As blood dripped from the broken spine onto the floor, the column of bone twisted and shook like a snake. X, fresh from showing off the grisly totem to Timmy-Tim, who had the notorious (and dead) bandit One Nose Clive chewing on his exposed intestinal tract, pulled Thomas in close. "Well, I guess this place is a bit screwed, but at least me and you got some special time huh?"

Thomas opened and closed his mouth, letting out a garbled call for brains once more. X pulled back his free hand, balled into a fist. The spinal cord curled up and lanced the jagged end into X's elbow, making him jump. In doing so, he instinctively bent his arm, which brought Thomas into contact with his face.

X let out a massive howl. Thomas was attached to his face, teeth grinding through stubbled cheek, managing to get into the bloody insides. X grabbed hold of the zombie's head and tried to pull it free, but its hold was total. It was then that he felt a hand run up the inside of his trousers, just above his boots.

Looking down, he saw Travis, near ripped apart by volley after volley of gunfire, but still in control of his hands and arms. With the trouser leg pulled apart, Travis snapped forward and bit into the back of X's calf. The pain made him stumble, and he collapsed to the floor. Travis worked his way up the leg, pulling and tearing out the workings of the limb.

Thomas, still clamped onto X's face, let go. Teeth clacked the air, drops of blood plinking into his open mouth. The gunfire had ceased. Now there was just the sound of slurping and meat being torn apart.

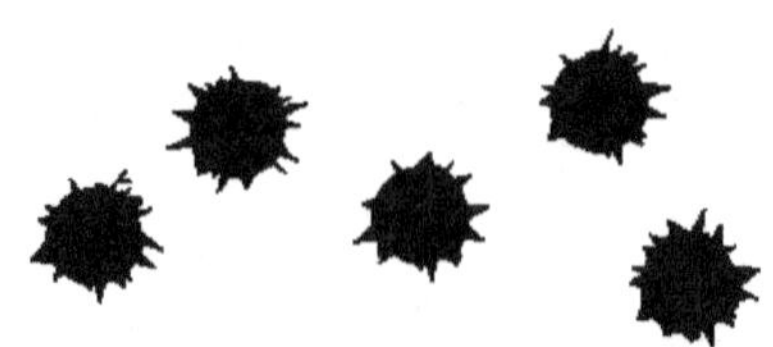

The groaning above the trap door had ceased a few hours back, or so Chad reckoned. When the place had turned into a blood bath, he had taken his leave and sequestered himself in the crawlspace beneath the bar. Daring to move, he saw the first rays of the morning sun creep up Main Street. After massaging some life back into his numb limbs, he made his way to the external wall and kicked a few of the wooden slats out, so he could finally taste freedom.

Silence had taken over the bar, but fear had held him hostage in the narrow gap beneath the feeding frenzy. Chad pulled down his sleeve and rubbed it on the glass. The scene within was nothing short of a butchers, an inept butchers who cared only about the hacking up of carcasses, and little of adequate storage and displaying their wares.

The town was silent. Chad stumbled aimlessly to its limits, looking to find some inspiration as to the next course of action. Should he leg it? Go to Van Horn and tell the sheriff? Would he even believe him if he did? As he contemplated what to do, he saw something move on the horizon.

Shielding the waking sun with his still shaking hands, he saw a wall of figures ambling off into the distance. A heat haze seemed to follow them in their wake. Chad shivered, his mind made up.

It didn't matter what he did, just so long as wherever *they* were going, he went in the opposite direction.

28 SECONDS LATER

May 7 1984

**Novogorsk district
Khimki Sports Preparation Facility**

"Comrade Slutsky, I trust your journey was amicable?" Doctor Yedlin enquired, holding his sweaty hand out to bid the Inspector welcome.

With a face seemingly carved from granite, Dmitri Slutsky peered down at the diminutive man and the proffered greeting. "Doctor, the taxi ride from my home to the train station was a nightmare. The driver you hired, seemingly intent on killing us both in an unsealed suicide pact.

"The eighteen hour train journey you arranged for me after, was hell manifested in reality. This is before I had experienced the so-called driving of the man you sent to ferry me from the station. He picked me up on a moped, which was ill prepared to hold my luggage. No doubt this has now been stolen and its contents sold around town.

"However, I would gladly do it all again than spend another second in that lift." Slutsky pointed to the rickety metal tube behind him, which, even after his departure, still shook and rattled.

Yedlin smiled nervously and wiped his hands over his lab coat. "Apologies, Inspector. When this facility was constructed, the Politburo thought it more prudent to spend the money on the laboratories than the lift. If it is any consolation, you do get used to it? In time…"

Slutsky ran a hand into his tightly closed jacket and retrieved a leather-bound notebook and stainless steel pen. Emphasising the point by clicking on the end of the pen, he scribbled inside the book, before replacing both back in their respective pocket. "No, Doctor, it is of no consolation. Whatsoever. Now, if we can attend to business? The games start in a little over three months, and I am yet to be convinced of the merit of your work. My superiors have demanded I report on its progress. Failure may result in certain personnel being…*relocated.*"

The doctor intercepted a bead of sweat which bloomed in his hairline. "*Relocated* you say? Somewhere tropical like Cuba? I've longed to see Havana in the summertime."

Slutsky leant in closer, nearly overpowering the man with the smell of cloves. "No. Siberia labour camp. Mining for salt."

Yedlin gulped. "I see. Well, there will be no need for that, I assure you Inspector. The final batch of athletes from our Warsaw Pact comrades arrived this very morning. They are all ready and waiting for their last round of injections and testing."

"Good, where shall we start?"

"Well, this facility is broken down into three sections. We have the track athletes down here, the field athletes, and all of their equipment behind you, with the weightlifters in the corridor behind young Boliakov there. Which do you fancy?"

Taking a few minutes to ponder, Slutsky thumbed to the corridor behind him. "Everyone can run and lift weights. I've always believed that the greatest skill lies in our field athletes. Shall we?"

Boliakov, the designated guard for the inspection, slapped his AK-47 a number of times, bringing the weapon finally to his shoulder. This merely received withering looks from Slutsky, who made another note in his book.

The central hub was perfectly circular, with a security office straddling the lift to the surface. The facility was stashed away under an abandoned playground, with rusting radiation signs keeping people out. The lift entrance above ground was cunningly hidden within a block of boarded up toilets.

An array of trolleys and sack trucks were shoved against the wall in the hub, having been used to transport all manner of athletic equipment into the underground facility the previous day.

Bordering each of the tunnels, which ran to their respective laboratories, were thick steel airlock doors, guarded around the clock by assault-rifle wielding soldiers. Everyone was issued with an ID card, which was required at all times, lest they incur the wrath of a barrage of 7.62mm rounds, ripping their body apart.

After running through the security checks with the guards, and signing in, the party of three were allowed admittance to the tunnel. Slutsky smirked, not sufficiently obvious for anyone to notice, but enough for his face to recognise muscles that were hardly ever used. Whilst his experience of the facility to date had been poor, as the door opened to reveal an impressive looking tunnel—complete with actual working lights and a gentle aroma of freshly cut flowers—it did start to fill him with his first sense that these so-called experts might actually know what they're doing.

Most of the establishments he inspected were little more than flea pits, with toilet facilities consisting of two buckets. With little or erratic lighting, many a time he had forced himself to stop mid-flow in order to prevent urinating on exposed wiring running through open floor panels. Needless to say that most of the people in charge of those buildings were now mining for Uranium in the Urals, with their bare tumour-ridden hands.

Each step was a metallic clang, echoed by the airlock door shutting behind them. The sudden change in pressure caused their ears to block up, plunging them into near silence. Slutsky breathed in, and felt as though nothing was actually being taken into his lungs. He looked across to Yedlin and Boliakov, who had their cheeks puffed out, holding their breath.

An air of desperation overtook him. He began to paw at the side of the tunnel, clutching his throat. The other two men saw him, rolled their eyes and placed an arm under an armpit, dragging him to the far end of the tunnel. After a near infinite opening cycle, a tiny opening offered some respite from the airless room.

With a hint of embarrassment, Yedlin said, "Apologies, Comrade. I forgot to mention that the access tunnels are devoid of oxygen, to aid with the full body scans. They're new. We're one of only two facilities to have installed them, you know."

Gasping in a lungful of air, Slutsky picked himself up off the floor, and feebly scrawled further notes in his book. "You could've told me first, you idiot. It is an unusual approach to try and asphyxiate the very person who controls your destiny. Scanning for what anyway?"

"Explosives predominantly, but also to make sure that no one removes any of the compounds that we make, either commercial adversaries or the Zionist agitators," Boliakov boomed proudly.

"Please, Comrade Slutsky, let us begin our tour. Just over here are the East German shot-put team," Yedlin suggested.

Having regained his poise, the inspector stood up to full height and took in another deep breath of air. Feeling rejuvenated, he nodded and followed the doctor. Boliakov fell in lockstep behind them. From the entrance to the section, metal corridors ran off into the distance. Large Plexiglas walls offered excellent views of the subjects within. "Ahhhh, I do enjoy the shot-put," Slutsky conceded.

Standing to attention, he surveyed the five people within. Muscles strained the very limits of their kit; shoulder straps near withered under bursting trapezius and deltoid muscles.

Within the sizable room, one athlete expertly hoisted the put nearly thirty metres. "Impressive work, though a bit much, wouldn't you say? If they did that in Los Angeles, surely everyone would suspect that they had received artificial assistance?"

Yedlin watched in awe. "Not at all, Comrade. Just because they can easily surpass the limits of other athletes, does not mean they will. Whilst we provide them with near limitless power, the coaches always tell them what distance they should be aiming for, so as to not raise suspicion."

Slutsky watched on as the athlete picked and pulled at their tracksuit trousers, which clung to the tree trunks masquerading as legs, "What fine young men they are indeed."

"Men?" Yedlin asked.

"Yes, men. I know that training in certain disciplines can sometimes blur gender distinction, but even I know that only men have Adam's apples," Slutsky barked back, pointing at the subjects' throats.

Boliakov stifled a laugh, then looked across to the Doctor, who blushed. "It is an…unfortunate side-effect of the formula that we have yet to correct, Comrade Slutsky. I think we have too much testosterone in there."

The Inspector fixed Yedlin a stern look. "You mean to tell me that these…are women?" he waved his hand across the glass, indicating the oblivious athletes inside.

"Erm…yes…Comrade," Yedlin replied nervously.

Slutsky pulled his notebook out once more. The pen scratched against the paper, and after a few moments, he said, "Fine…please see to it that this oversight is corrected. If I can discern the difference so easily, so will the entire world, doctor. Do you want the glorious motherland ridiculed and shamed?"

"No, Comrade," Yedlin replied weakly.

"Good, now, what's next?"

"I thought I would show you the laboratory itself, where we keep the formula? We've just created a new batch, and it is ready for injection. I thought you would like to see it administered, first hand?"

With an arm outstretched, Doctor Yedlin led the way, walking past more athletes of gender unknown, performing acts of track splendour which defied traditional measurement. There was a clang as a javelin became lodged in the ceiling, the result of an over-exuberant throw. The Plexiglas strained as a discus shot out of the back of a Hungarian athlete's hand, causing spider webs of cracks to run up the thick material.

"That's odd," Yedlin mumbled as they approached the main laboratory.

"What is it now?" Slutsky asked.

"There should be two guards outside each entrance, but they're not here…and that ceiling panel shouldn't be ajar either. What is that shuriken doing embedded in the wall?" Yedlin pointed out.

Boliakov jogged past the men and searched the area. He opened up a large plastic chest and slung his rifle over his shoulder. "Doctor, come quickly, look."

Yedlin and Slutsky exchanged nervous glances, before power-walking down the corridor to the young soldier, who was leaning over the box. As they got to him, Yedlin put a hand over his mouth. "Good god, are they? Are they dead?" he asked.

With a finger on one of the unconscious men's jugular, Boliakov shook his head. "No sir, they are both knocked out. I'd say from the abrasion on their necks, that it was some kind of Judo chop."

"Judo chop?" Slutsky asked, incredulously.

"Or Karate, Comrade, I can't work out which, but they were both knocked out by someone who is proficient in martial arts."

The Inspector sighed. "And pray tell, Private Boliakov, how do you know that?"

Boliakov undid his top button and showed the man his bruised shoulder. "First-hand experience, sir. We get these all the time from our unarmed training courses."

"But why did they climb into the box together? Did they not realise that this is not the time, nor the place, for homosexual communion?" Yedlin asked.

Slutsky sighed. "Good Doctor, these men did not climb in here together, they were knocked out and cast into the crate. We have an intruder."

Turning red, the doctor bellowed, "This base is as secure as the Kremlin! How dare you Slutsky! I will be reporting you to—"

Boliakov tapped Yedlin on the shoulder, and pointed through the safety glass, into the laboratory. "Sorry sir, but he's right. Look."

The three men peered into the room, and saw a man wearing an immaculate tuxedo with slicked back hair, Kung-Fu chopping a scientist. "Ahhh, of course, Kung-Fu," Boliakov said, bringing his rifle up to his shoulder. "Leave this to me."

A theatrical hiss from the door opened it into the corridor, and the three men entered just as the intruder adjusted his bulky cufflinks. Yedlin and Slutsky moved behind a worktop, littered with empty beakers and metal trays.

Unaware he had company, the man picked up a vial of bubbling green liquid and held it up to the light. "I am the walrush, *goo-goo*-ga-choo," he said with a Scottish lilt.

"Don't move, Amerikos," Boliakov ordered, levelling his rifle at the man's back.

Slowly, the man raised his hands, still holding the vial. "How dare you! Don't you know that I'm Shcottish? Shay, do you mind, if I turn around at leasht?"

"Okay, but slowly, or I'll…blow you away," Boliakov replied.

"As you shay, Mishter Cagney."

The man turned around, revealing a cheeky grin. "My god," Slutsky said. "It's international spy, and renowned fornicator, Percy D'Anger."

"The very shame," D'Anger replied, winking.

"What are you doing here?" Slutsky demanded

"Shay now, I'm just here on Her Majeshty's requesht, making shure you Rushkies were playing fair." Percy waved the bubbling tube. "Looksh like you weren't, old chap."

D'Anger looked across to the nervous soldier and began to lower his hands. "Now, boy, how about you lower that rifle and we can all have a little chat. You besht get back to your paper round, or you'll take shomeone's eye out with that."

Boliakov looked puzzled, and hesitated, long enough to allow D'Anger to aim a super-spy cufflink at the soldier. In one fluid motion, he pressed a button underneath the cufflink. A red laser beam shot out and caught Boliakov square in the throat. As he clamped his free hand over the smoking wound, his other hand, holding the AK-47, fell free, his finger pulled the trigger.

A slew of bullets stitched a diagonal row, starting with an unconscious scientist through a computer monitor, before the last three rounds hit the spy in the chest. "My god…you're not shupposed to shoot me! Missh Foxshy wash expecting me…for shome shex, schampagne and shmoked shalmon shandwiches…" Percy drawled, before falling to the floor in stages. He was, however, beaten by the dead body of Boliakov, who slammed into a counter and, after a shower of teeth chips, hit the floor.

The vial tumbled out of Percy's hand and smashed against the floor. The liquid within turned into an acrid green vapour as it came into contact with oxygen. The powerful air conditioning unit pulled it upwards, creating a thin coned tornado as it was sucked up into the ceiling ducts.

Slutsky trotted over to the spy and cautiously felt for a pulse. "He's…dead…rather easily too. Do you know how many times we've had him cornered, only for him to escape? Implausibly?"

Ignoring him, Yedlin walked over to where the final wisp of vapour was pulled up into the air conditioning unit. Slutsky pulled out his pen and notebook once more. "At last, Comrade, I have something good to report back to your superiors at your inevitable tribunal."

Yedlin shushed him and cocked his ear. "What's that noise?"

"I don't he—"

A raised finger from the doctor silenced the man; even his notetaking ceased. From outside in the corridor, a klaxon wailed. Like a Mexican wave, the sirens in the laboratory kicked into gear, before passing the baton to the neighbouring tunnel.

"What's going on, Comrade?" Slutsky asked, casting nervous glances around the room.

Yedlin dashed over to a computer panel, and with the CRT screen reflecting off his glasses, he began to pore through various reports. The data he saw made him swear at a rate hitherto unknown. Slutsky stood over him, trying to make sense of the reams of data, eventually losing his temper and blurting out, "FOR GOD'S SAKE MAN, TELL ME!"

The doctor had turned white. He pointed a trembling finger at the large screen above the console. "Watch this." With one keystroke, grainy CCTV footage blinked into life on a screen usually reserved for showing graphs and fluctuating charts.

The images were from one of the athlete modules. The five subjects, who evidently were planning on competing in the hammer throw, were practising their sport. Though instead of using the regulation Olympic hammer, they were utilising the spinal columns and skulls of the scientists who had been monitoring their progress.

"Erm…" Slutsky mumbled.

"I know," Yedlin said.

Slutsky squinted at the screen. "Are they women? I can't really tell from this angle."

"Damn you, Inspector. Can't you see what they're doing?" Yedlin pointed to a Bulgarian, who, after beating his personal best using the entrails of Doctor Uminov, was now kneeling over the steaming remains of the old man, tucking into one of his kidneys.

Yedlin tapped some more. Another camera feed popped into life on the big screen. "It's the athletics lab…" he pointed out. The camera was affixed at the far end of one of the access tunnels, above a security station. At the top of the picture was a soldier, his clothes torn. Even with the crappy inbuilt microphones, his screaming was as loud as a banshee who had caught her fingers in a door. The soldier bolted, full pelt, towards the lens, trying desperately to get to the door beneath the camera.

"Go on, Comrade, you can do it," Yedlin said, willing him on.

Slutsky reached into his pocket and pulled out his wallet. He lay a twenty-ruble note on the console. "Twenty says he doesn't make it."

The soldier, still bawling and hollering, was getting bigger and bigger on the screen. Yedlin asked, "What makes you so cocksure?"

"That." Slutsky pointed to a figure who was chasing the man down. It looked human, and was dressed in a Hungarian tracksuit and vest combination. However, he was traversing the ground at around the same speed a cheetah bolts after an antelope. His arms were pumping up and down like a pair of hyperactive pistons.

Despite having a head start of fifty feet, the soldier, perfectly framed in shot, was tackled from behind by the speeding athlete. There was a yelp and a whimper, before the Hungarian knelt down and ripped out the soldier's throat. "Holy shit," Yedlin shouted. "Did you see how fast he went?"

Slutsky nodded. "Look, even the fatties can motor." He pointed to another camera shot, where the Russian 110kg Weightlifter, Igor 'The Bear' Chekov, was chasing down a female scientist, who was trying to get away on a motorised cart.

Yedlin reluctantly made the image appear on the main screen. The woman, who he recognised as Svetlana Rekova, weaved in and out of piles of unfortunately placed barrels. The Bear smashed the containers out of his way, as if they were small children in an ice cream queue, catching the cart up with ease. Having reached the back of the vehicle, he picked it up as if it were nothing more than a toy truck, and hurled it against the wall. Svetlana, dazed and concussed, crawled out of the wreckage, only to be set upon by a Polish bantamweight athlete, who stood on the unfortunate woman's back and pulled both of her arms out of their sockets.

After that, she stopped moving, started bleeding, and was eaten alive by a horde of rather beefy weightlifters.

Slutsky retrieved his notebook and pen. "So…Doctor Anton Yedlin, would you be so bold as to tell me what exactly is in that formula of yours?"

Yedlin gulped. "It's nothing…just the usual mix of steroids, formaldehyde, fluoride, testosterone, E24 and a hint of vodka. Actually, less of a hint, and more of a solid backbone of vodka. It's the only thing that keeps the rest in check."

"What else?"

The doctor coyly swung his leg. "Maybe some radioactive isotopes from the sturdy nuclear facility at Chernobyl."

The Inspector slapped Yedlin across the face. "Your kind are always the same. You know you shouldn't meddle with the make-up of man, but you always have to go and take it one step too far, don't you? Seriously, what is it with you scientists and radioactivity?"

Collecting himself and, after checking to see if he had lost any teeth, Yedlin answered weakly. "It's what gives it the extra kick. We were floundering before we tried it. We had the Kremlin threatening us with being used as firing squad practice, or as rabbits for their Alsation training. What were we supposed to do? They needed results, *impossible* results. To do that, we had to *do* the impossible."

Slutsky sighed. "I guess I can't blame you for that." He looked up at the screen as the 4x100m Russian men's relay team sprinted after the last of the guards in their block, and brought him down. Like a pack of hyenas, they sat around the carcass, tearing off strips of flesh and growling at each other. Then a thought hit him. "Hang on. Why have they gone like this now? Surely they would've done so before, when you injected them."

Yedlin took off his glasses. "When we first tried it, this happened…luckily it was an isolated case, and we were able to destroy the specimen. Then we learnt that the compound needs to be mixed with a stabiliser for it to be contained. That damn fool D'Anger released the undiluted formula into the air ducts. Anyone who has been injected has had an overdose. It won't affect us, you see."

"What about this…patient zero? What symptoms did they have? We need to know what we're up against," Slutsky said.

"Well, first off, Inspector, they are to all intents and purposes, still human…"

"But why in the name of Gorbachev's head splodge are they eating people alive? You don't think they're…no, I feel silly saying it."

"I know what you're going to say, Inspector, please don't."

"Zombies. They're goddamn zombies, aren't they?" Slutsky yelled.

Yedlin squashed his face with his hands. "They can't be zombies, Comrade. They're not dead! Look, they were fine one minute, and then…what…28 seconds later—"

"28 seconds? That's awfully precise."

"Please, allow me to finish. 28 seconds later, they became *infected*. They are not dead, they are *infected*. The prerequisite for being a zombie is that you need to be dead. Infected does not mean zombified; there is a clear distinction, scientifically speaking, between the two states. Zombie. Infected. Zombie. Infected. It is evident to even the simplest of village idiot," Yedlin argued.

"In Haiti, zombies are still alive. In fact—"

Yedlin pointed at the stampeding athletes. "But zombies don't run! We've all seen the films smuggled in from America, pure and simple fact. Zombies. Do. Not. Run. Sir, I appreciate your viewpoint, but I do not think this is the time or place to debate what constitutes a member of the undead."

Slutsky pointed a gloved finger at the screen, as world-renowned decathlete, Yuri Rimmikov, swallowed whole the liver of a still twitching guard. "These are quite clearly zombies, dead or no, they're eating people."

Yedlin held out his hands in defense. "Sir, please, can we just agree to disagree? I know, some people, such as you, will think they're zombies, whilst others, me included, do not. It doesn't matter. What does is that they are infused with superhuman strength and speed.

"Before we managed to euthanise the original specimen, he managed to do the one hundred metres in just under five seconds. Just to get to one of the interns we had in for a few months, who was helping us out with some data crunching. They were one day away from having their contract renewed. One. Day."

"What happened to him?"

"He got…crunched…and we hired someone else. In truth, they had better data crunching experience, having worked at—"

Slutsky slapped Yedlin again. "Enough of that. We had all the potential silliness from that blasted spy D'Anger. I don't need it from you."

The Doctor nodded. "Fair point. Well made, Comrade."

"Any thoughts on how we deal with this mess of yours, doctor?"

Spinning back to the computer console, Yedlin tapped away furiously before bringing up a slowly rotating 3D-vector graphic blueprint of the base. "Wow, that looks really futuristic," Slutsky commented.

"This facility is built at the bottom of an old ICBM silo. Though they took the rockets away, the warheads are still down here with us, in…this section right here."

Slutsky pulled his hand back, making the doctor flinch. "Are you suggesting that we annihilate the entire Eastern Bloc's athletic teams, three months before our chance to show the Imperialist pigdogs who is better? We have waited since their cowardice at the Moscow Olympics, bided our time to show them who the true kings of track and field are."

Yedlin began to sob, at the threat of impending violence, and at the thought of his insides being pulled out. "Well, we have to do something, look." The doctor tapped into another camera feed. "There aren't many soldiers left. Once they've devoured them all, and pooped, they'll then break through the airlocks to the service elevator. From there, they will be eating and infecting their way through the entire country in a few hours."

Slumped against a chair, Slutsky rolled his eyes, and looked at the crackly images of an infected Russian high jumper finishing off the leg of a soldier, tearing at it as if it were a piece of cooked chicken. Another sat close by, pulling out the ligaments from a particularly stringy lab assistant. "Wait…look at them."

Yedlin sighed and gazed at the images, suppressing the bile burning the back of his throat. All he could see were his colleagues and one time canteen chatters, being ripped apart by freakishly proportioned mutants. "Yes, and?"

Slutsky pointed at the athletes, sat mere inches apart, sharing a spinal column, teasing morsels of marrow out. "They're not attacking each other, only those who aren't the same as them."

"That is all well and good, Comrade, but if you bother to look in a mirror, you'll see that we aren't the same as them, are we?" Yedlin snapped back.

Sighing, Slutsky waited for the doctor's brain to catch up, which took longer than it should; he put it down to shock. Finally Yedlin clicked his fingers. "Of course! If we take an injection of stimulants, we should be like them."

"Will we turn into those slathering fools out there?"

Yedlin shook his head. "We shouldn't. They only turned when the undiluted formula was pumped through the air conditioning. If we purge the pipes, it should be clear. So, we'll inject ourselves with the formula, then head to the basement to get the nuclear warhead, prime it, and then get out of here in the lift. What could possibly go wrong?"

Slutsky pointed to the skeletal remains of the facilities staff on the camera images. "Quite, Comrade, what could possibly go wrong?"

Ignoring him, the Doctor rooted around in a fridge, and found two prepared shots of the super-formula, ready loaded into applicator guns. Slutsky rolled his sleeve up and looked at Yedlin, whose hands were shaking. "Are you okay to do this?"

"Yeah…fine…"

Yedlin plugged the end against the Inspector's arm and pressed the trigger, shooting the frigid green goo into the man's arm. "It tingles," Slutsky said, with a hint of surprise.

"Brace yourself, Comrade, for this next bit may sting a little."

Laughing at the sheer incredulity of the man's words, Slutsky's smile disappeared quickly as he felt tendrils of fire race through every nerve-ending and muscle in his body. He flung his head back, the veins in his neck corded; it looked like a thick church candle with melted wax globules running down the side. "It…it…it…hurts…" he managed to say through teeth gritted together so tightly that he feared he might grind them into powder.

"That's not even the worst bit yet, Comrade," Yedlin replied.

With a look of surprise, Slutsky wondered what in hell could be worse than the searing pain and agony he was currently experiencing.

Then it happened. Every fibre of his being started to balloon, as muscles and the associated cardio-vascular infrastructure began to grow. This process was far from consistent though, and Slutsky could feel the insides of his body pressing against his skeleton.

Organs bulged through his rib cage, threatening to burst open. He could feel his heart beat so fast, it felt like it was going to begin a career as a professional pogo jumper. His eyes pulsed and fluttered, pushing against the confines of his sockets. He dared to look down at his arms, and saw the flesh ripple beneath the skin as muscle swelled and formed underneath. With a sideways glance at the doctor, he saw that Yedlin too was starting to undergo the change.

The pair of them thrashed around on the floor, as the metamorphosis wracked their bodies with vast amounts of chemicals. They counted their lucky stars as unconsciousness claimed them.

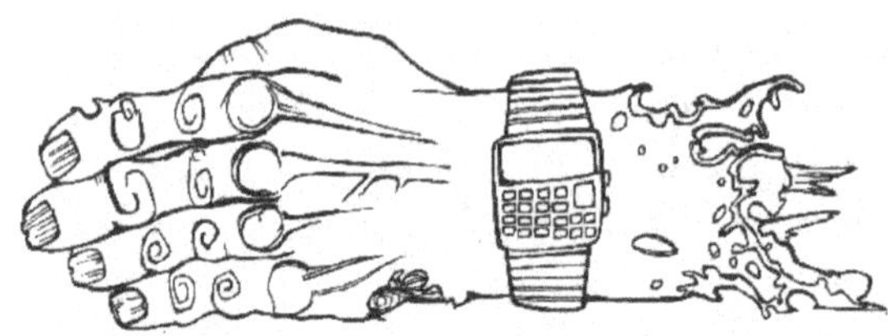

They came to as a loud thudding rang through their ears. At first, Slutsky thought it was his head pounding, a side effect of his brain expanding against the skull tomb it was imprisoned within. Then he realised that it was the main door. Standing up, which made the ground beneath him spin, he saw a blonde haired man in a Polish vest, with a gore streaked chin, pummelling the steel door.

What the manufacturers touted as 'bomb proof' was evidently not enough to stop a mutated freakazoid, hopped up on an insane cocktail of hormones and steroids. The hinges were beginning to buckle, and after a few more lusty blows, the door gave up the ghost and fell into the room, slamming against the floor with a showy cloud of dust. Slutsky felt a hand on his arm and looked sideways, expecting to see Yedlin there.

What stood next to him was a facsimile of the doctor, but one that appeared to have been given a fancy dress costume with added padding. He was a good six inches taller than before, and whereas his arms used to be nothing more than skin wrapped around bone, they were now rippling limbs of barely contained crushing power. His clothing was ragged, as it had come apart at the seams following the transformation. He stood there in tattered remains of a shirt, now classified as a vest, and a pair of trousers, nothing more than a pair of cut off shorts.

Yedlin coughed, looked at the Inspector and whispered, "Quit looking at me like that. You're dressed the same." Slutsky looked down to see that if it wasn't for his pant elastic, he would be naked from his newly acquired six pack down. The Doctor put a finger to his lips, and pointed at the bloodied freak. "Don't. Do. Anything."

The Polish athlete galloped through the breach and into the room. He picked up the corpse of Percy D'Anger and, after sniffing the crotch, flung the body against the wall, which made a rather enchanting sound of ground bone and splats of congealed blood. After checking the other bodies in similar fashion, he bounded up to the two men.

Its face was right in theirs, nostrils flared like a hyper-puckering sphincter as it sniffed the pair. Yedlin looked into the crazed eyes of the pole-vault world record holder; stringy pieces of vein hung from his chin like a thick straggly beard. After a couple of deep breaths in, the Pole flicked his head to the side and scampered back down the tunnel he had just come from, growling and hooting along the way.

Slutsky relaxed a little. "At least we know that it has worked…"

"For now, yes, though there is something else lurking inside them. They seem driven by base instinct, but I can see a hint of intelligence within them still. We should be cautious," Yedlin warned.

"I think you worry too much, doctor. Now, let's go. We don't have much time before the zombies run out of meal options and try to make their way to the surface," Slutsky said.

"But they're not zom—"

"Huh?"

"Never mind, Inspector. Let's go."

Picking their way back down the tunnel to the central hub, they inched past crouched athletes. Once considered to be the best of the best, they were now nothing more than cannibals, scraping the last morsels from the bones of the slaughtered guards.

A Czechoslovakian discus athlete wrenched free a scapula from one of the poor sods, and tested its aerodynamics by flinging it down the hallway. Slutsky ducked underneath it and whispered to Yedlin, "What are they doing?"

"Some kind of instinct. Memory, of what they used to do. This was an important thing in their lives. They don't know why…they just remember," the doctor replied. The feeding pack, a few sniffs aside, ignored them, and continued to feast on the steaming carcasses.

Finally, they managed to scramble over the last of the debris and assorted body parts, and reached the central hub. A number of the infected were milling around the lift. Some even stood inside its metal cage, slapping the chicken wire as if trying to instil some life into the machine. From out of nowhere, a soldier ran screaming down the weightlifting tunnel, and straight into the arms of Yedlin. The soldier, gore streaked and dishevelled, bounced off the doctor's taut torso and slammed into the floor.

All of the mutants began to growl and stomp towards what could be the last piece of warm flesh left in the facility. The soldier, Viktor Grabev, stood up on uneasy legs and looked at Yedlin and Slutsky. "Hey…you two look different. You don't look like the rest of these freaks."

"Shut up," Slutsky hissed.

"Come on, Comrade, you gotta help me. I saw one of them pull Alexei's head off as if it were the lid to a jar of pickled cheese. I don't want to die, you gotta help me. Please!"

By now, the ruckus was attracting attention from the inhabitants of the central hub, who were stalking the mid-morning snack. One of them, a Polish long jumper called Piotr Michal, slapped Yedlin on the back, pushing him towards the man. Yedlin looked back at Slutsky, who, wide eyed, was staring at the soldier, blinking, and then down at his own clawed hands. After seconds of dumb confusion, the doctor finally worked out what he meant. "But I can't, Comrade," he whispered.

Michal pushed Yedlin again, growling at him more fiercely, jabbing a finger at the mewling man, a digit the same size as a prize Frankfurter.

"If we don't…they'll know we're not like them. Do it. Gut the poor bastard," Slutsky hissed through clenched teeth.

Yedlin stood up tall and looked down at the man, who by now had backed up into the doctor's abdomen, using it as a shelter from the impending rending of skin and bone. "I'm sorry," Yedlin said. A look of surprise coated the soldier's face as the doctor clamped his hands around his skull and lifted him off the floor with no trouble at all.

"B…b…b…" the man slobbered, his skull contracting under the pressure.

Then, as the first fractures appeared within the internal structure of his skull, the soldier's head exploded like a melon in a rubbish compactor. Yedlin was sprayed with blood, worms of brain, and shards of bone, as the entire skull disintegrated. He was left holding the man by the tip of his spinal column.

Satisfied, Michal grabbed hold of the soldier's spasming leg and snatched the body from Yedlin, who looked down into his blood-slick hands. The infected descended onto the corpse, but before they began they looked up to the two men expectantly. Slutsky coughed, and nodded towards the twitching corpse. "Come on, you have to join in. It's your kill."

Resigned to the inevitability, Yedlin crouched down, taking his place amongst his uncouth dinner guests. He looked the body up and down, and opted to make it easy for himself. As he suppressed the urge to lose his morning coffee all over his victim, he reached into the exposed neck cavity and rooted around with his fingers.

It was slippery, and he couldn't get a decent hold of anything, which just incurred more growling and jostling from his mutant feeding buddies. Deciding it was now or never, he shoved his hand further into the ragged wound, ending up elbow deep and with his fingers firmly ensconced within the chest cavity. He felt something warm and bulbous. His fingers dug into it and gained some purchase. With a gentle tug, which belied his strength, he pulled out a pair of lungs, holding them up like a large bunch of grapes.

This seemed to impress some of the pack, who cooed and dribbled in acknowledgement at such a prize hunk of meat. As dozens of pairs of baleful eyes looked at him, Yedlin lowered a lung into his mouth, and despite every ounce of his being screaming at him to stop, took a huge bite. After a few chews, Yedlin opened his eyes and saw that his infected chums—satisfied that the hunter had eaten first—were tucking in with wilful abandon.

It didn't actually taste that bad. Most of the meals Yedlin had eaten through his life were tepid stews, filled with rock hard vegetables and meat of dubious origin. He walked over to Slutsky, still ripping off lengths of fibrous lung. "You want some?" he asked the Inspector. Instinctively, Slutsky reached for his jacket pocket, no doubt to write up yet another infraction, only to discover that it was no longer there.

The Inspector tapped his head. "No matter. I will remember this."

"But you told me to blend in," Yedlin protested, though his words were barely audible, as he tried to break up chewy lengths of worm-like bronchi with his teeth.

"Can we go and do what we need to? Unless you'd like to stay here and sample some more?"

Yedlin held his hands up; the lung swung in the air like a meat pendulum. "I'm good. Let's get going."

They started to walk towards the cellar hatch when Slutsky pointed to the hunk of meat still in Yedlin's hands. "Are you going to get rid of that?"

Reluctantly, and after taking one last huge bite, Yedlin threw the remnants of the organ to the feeding mob, who snatched it gladly.

The hatch was open. After checking that nothing and no-one was coming up the ladder, the pair descended into the confines of the basement. It was used as storage for any of the crap that the facility no longer needed, much like an attic in most people's houses.

Amongst empty cardboard boxes for electrical equipment, and piles of moth eaten blankets, Slutsky unearthed a large wooden crate, which had the eponymous radiation symbol branded onto its surface. "Subtle," Yedlin quipped, invoking another tap on the side of his head by the Inspector, as if it contained some kind of recording equipment.

Slutsky dug his fingernails under the lip of the lid and lifted it free, as if it were a sheet of paper. The pair looked into the bowels of the crate, and saw something covered by another khaki blanket. With a quick tug, Yedlin revealed the nuclear warhead beneath, even adding in a shallow bow to an imaginary audience. Turning to Slutsky, he asked, "Do you know what you've got to do?"

The Inspector was already picking through an overly complicated wad of wires and computer chips, delving deeper into the brain of the device. After a number of "Oooohhhs," and "Ahhhhhhs," Slutsky held up a powered-down digital display. "This here is the timer, which we would've been able to set to detonate, and ensure that we have enough time to reach minimum safe distance."

Yedlin paused. "Are you using the past tense intentionally?"

Slutsky nodded. "Unfortunately, yes. The timer is broken. It means that one of us will have to stay behind and activate the warhead manually."

"Ah…"

"Precisely, doctor."

There was a slight pause, bordering on awkward, before Yedlin asked, "So, how do we do this? Draw lots? Test each other's scientific acumen?"

Slutsky smiled. "I was thinking paper, rock, scissors, Comrade."

"Fine, let's get this done," the doctor conceded.

"1…2…3…" Slutsky said, forming his hand into a rock which, given its artificial enhancement, would've been categorised as a decent sized meteor.

"Dammit," Yedlin said, his fingers having turned into a blunt pair of scissors.

"Unlucky, Comrade."

Yedlin sighed, "Best of three?"

"Very well. 1…2…3…." Slutsky made another rock, matched by the doctor. "Oh…a draw…"

"Not quite, Comrade," Yedlin added. With a speed only made real by the varied concoction of chemicals now running rampant in his body, Yedlin smacked Slutsky square in the face, breaking his nose.

With the Inspector dumped onto his arse on the floor, the doctor placed one foot above the stunned man's knee, pinning him to the ground. Then, after interlocking his fingers, he placed his hands underneath Slutsky's heel. With a sickening crack, Yedlin pulled the leg up, going completely against the anatomical design set down by evolution for thousands of years.

Slutsky screamed in pain. Daring to look, he gazed upon the sole of his foot for the first time ever. Yedlin let go and took a step backwards, out of being-punched-in-the-happy-sack range. "I'm sorry, Comrade, really, I am, but you left me no choice."

Chewing on his tongue to suppress the waves of agony, Slutsky looked up at Yedlin. "Fine…I guess it will be me that activates the nuclear warhead."

"Thank you, Comrade. I really apprec—"

"You have five minutes, Comrade. If you're not out of the silo by then, I believe that your skin will slough off your bones as it is melted to a million degrees."

Yedlin opened and closed his mouth, no words coming out, but eventually he mustered, "But…that's…"

"Four minutes, fifty seconds, Comrade. May I suggest you start to get out of here. Unless you want me to set it off now?"

The doctor spun on his heels and leapt onto the ladder, taking it two rungs at a time. "Thank you, Comrade," he shouted down into the basement.

Pulling himself up into the central hub, he saw that the other mutants were now trying to work out how to use the lift. Yedlin pushed his way through the throng and got into the metal cage, which doubled up as an elevator.

Above him he saw a hatch, and knew what he had to do. Punching it open, he clambered over a Russian pentathlete, and hung from the hole in the roof. He kicked out and crushed the lift controls with the heel of his foot. Once on top of the lift, he slammed the hatch closed and bent the bars together, so it formed a tight lattice of metal, which not even Houdini would've escaped from in time.

Looking above him, the shaft loomed overhead. A saucer of light shone from the top, signalling the way out. Grabbing hold of the thick steel cable, he clambered up it like an experienced pirate, shimmying up the main mast to the crow's nest. As he neared the top, he heard a rumble of thunder beneath him. Not daring to look down, Yedlin put every ounce of effort into climbing up the cable to freedom.

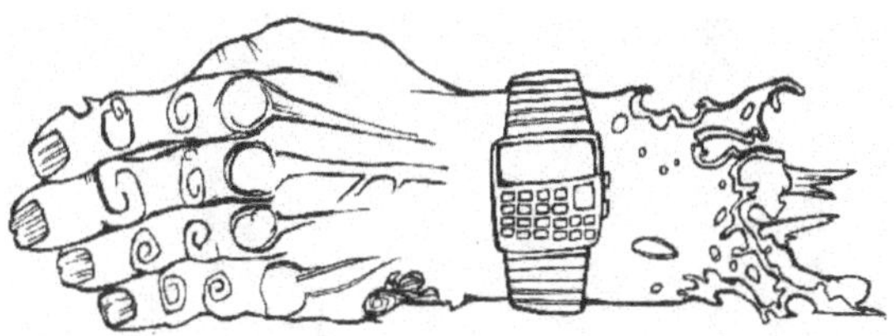

"In today's Seoul Olympics news, despite being plagued by accusations of doping, Russian weightlifter, Anton Yedlin, easily claimed the gold medal, lifting a new personal best, and world record.

"The secretive man, once rumoured to be a scientist and keen racketball enthusiast, dedicated it to, 'The true heroes of Mother Russia,' cryptically adding, 'and to those who know the difference between infected and zombies.'

"Back to you in the studio, Mike."

RED SABRE ONE

"Red Sabre One, this is Sabre Command, do you copy?"

Captain Ferguson raised a clenched fist. As one, the four-man team sunk to their knees. Like a bristling hedgehog, each weapon was brought up to bear. "This is Red Sabre One, I copy." Each man wore black combat trousers and assault vests, emotionless gas-mask-covered faces scanned the dimly-lit corridor they had made their way into.

The headset crackled into life again. "Red Sabre One, give me a sitrep."

Ferguson checked to make sure there was no movement ahead, before signalling to Trooper Neil 'Smudger' Smith to cover him. "Sabre Command, we are approaching the egress. Minimal contacts so far. I thought you said that this place was swarming with Tangos?"

Smudger's blank masked face looked at the Captain and made the wanker hand motion. Ferguson ran a finger across his throat and pointed to the door ahead of them. Smudger nodded languidly and resumed overwatch.

"Red Sabre One, Tangos have broken through the main gate and have blockaded the principal X-Ray's main entrance. From the survivors who made it out of Whitehall, they said that it was full of people. Keep your eyes peeled; they have to be there somewhere."

"Affirmative. Red Sabre One, out." Ferguson cut the comms and pulled his MP5 sub-machine gun into his shoulder. He scanned the way ahead. "Okay you lot, let's get this done. Spud, get the frame charge ready. We'll breach into the stairwell, and get down to the basement door, clear?"

A round of monosyllabic replies sounded off through their ear-pieces. With a hand gesture from Ferguson, the squad edged towards the door. They had rehearsed this so many times that it was now second nature. As two men covered their backs, Spud affixed the frame charge to the door, whilst Smudger kept watch.

"Ready," Spud grunted into his mic. The two men by the door took a few steps back and braced themselves. Smudger pulled a flashbang grenade from his belt and waited.

The charge exploded and punched a perfectly rectangular hole through the door. No sooner had the breach been made than Smudger pulled the pin and lobbed the grenade into the miasma formed by the explosion. A deafening bang rippled through the men, followed by a blinding light, which none of them witnessed having shielded their eyes.

With the noise still ringing in their ears, Spud pulled his MP5 up and entered the stairwell, yelling, "Clear," down the mic as he saw there was nothing on the other side. Red Sabre Team worked their way down the stairs like a lethal slinky. At the bottom, they checked a deserted security post for signs of life. The emergency lighting pasted a sickly glow over the whitewashed walls, casting long shadows from the most mundane of objects.

Ferguson rolled over a table usually reserved for rooting through handbags and briefcases and paced towards a large bank-vault-like door, complete with large metal wheel. The rest of the team formed up. With Smudger and Spud watching their backs, Ferguson and Denny stood either side of the door.

"Sabre Command, we are at the airlock door, preparing to enter. Radio blackout will persist until we're through the tunnel."

Ferguson nodded, and Denny slung his weapon over his shoulder and began to turn the metal wheel to unseal the lock. As it popped out of its thick frame, a bassy moan washed over the men. Denny heaved the door open and Ferguson switched on the light under the gun barrel.

"Fuck, looks like we've found the survivors," Ferguson reported. The heavy door thudded into the concrete wall and the other members of Red Sabre Team turned towards the corridor, adding their beams of light to the glow.

During peacetime, the tunnel acted as a quick conduit from the Ministry of Defence to Downing Street, for ministers and civil servants alike. To allay any concerns of terrorist attack, the tunnel itself, over a hundred feet in length, was completely airtight. Once you were in, you hoped to everything you held dear that the security guard on the other end was ready and waiting for you.

Torchlights ran over dozens of grey faces. Some were sitting down, as if attending a minimalist picnic, whilst others pawed at the smooth concrete walls. As soon as the door opened, the entombed survivors, whose oxygen supply had long since been used up when they were sealed in, opened their mouths and staggered towards dinner.

"Poor bastards," Denny muttered, invoking a blank stare from the Captain.

"Gents, advance and clear," Ferguson barked. With the Scotsman and Denny hunched over, Smudger and Spud stood a few paces behind them. The four men moved purposefully forward.

The suppressors reduced every shot to a muffled 'thwap', but each round slammed into the skull of the advancing horde of smartly dressed zombies. As they made their way into the tunnel, the men had to walk over the dead bodies, laid out like a deep pile carpet.

"There are too many of them," Denny shrieked over the radio.

Ferguson smacked him on the arm and shouted back, "Stay focused, fire and move. We're nearly through."

The undead horde surged towards the first hint of food they had seen since reanimation, but their advances were slowed by their slain kin. "I'm empty," Spud called out. He let his MP5 swing around his body. He pulled out his P226 pistol, allowing no let-up in the mass extinction event going on thirty feet below the road above, also awash with the newly risen dead.

"There, the exit is up ahead," Ferguson said. His sub-machine gun empty, he too swapped to his handgun, and continued the merciless assault.

As the last of the zombified civil servants collapsed to the ground, Red Sabre Team picked up the pace and jogged to the end. "Arrrgggghhhh," Denny screamed. Ferguson turned around and saw the newbie ankle deep in dead bodies. He shone his light over the macabre rug, and saw a grey arm wrapped around the man's leg, "It's fucking got me," Denny shouted.

Ferguson pushed past Smudger and Spud, thumbing towards the doorway ahead. They nodded and left the Captain to it. By the time he got to Denny, the young man was thrashing around as if stuck in quicksand.

Denny looked down into the vacant eyes of a woman, who could've been quite the looker when she was alive. Her make-up was now smeared over her face, the pallor of her skin akin to gone off ham. She clawed at his trousers with sparkly red painted nails. Despite her acrylic talons and keenness to feast on the young man's groin, she was unable to tear through the thick material.

As he looked into those orbs of nothingness, her head rocked backwards. The scratching on his thigh ceased as a perfectly round hole was stamped on her forehead. She slumped backwards and joined the rest of the slaughtered zombies. Ferguson smacked Denny on top of his combat helmet. "Get your head back in the game, son, or I'll fucking leave you here with your fan club."

Denny softly nodded. "Yes, Sir, sorry, I…I don't know what happened."

"I don't give a fuck. We've got a job to do, and we don't have time for your pissy pant bullshit, now get the fuck over there," Ferguson bellowed, pointing to the two men who were burning through the thick metal door's hinges with a thermal lance. Denny stood up straight, reloaded and stormed over to the rest of the team.

"Stand back," Spud warned, as the thick door wobbled under its own weight and lurched back into the corridor. The top landed on the skull of one of the despatched office workers spraying the walls in lumps of brain and congealed blood, as if a truck had driven through a puddle of gore.

With each man having replenished their weapons ammunition, Ferguson took point and stepped through the doorway into the stairwell beyond. Like the one they had just left, it too had an unguarded security desk and a set of stairs leading to the gloom above.

"…abre One, do you copy?"

Ferguson pushed the intercom button. "Copy Sabre Command, we're in the basement of number ten now."

"Good work, Red Sabre One. Did you find the survivors?"

Ferguson stood at the bottom of the stairs. As the rest of the team carefully ascended, he looked back at the tunnel packed with the wilted dead. "Affirmative, Sabre Command, they're gone. All of them. We're moving up to get the principal X-Ray. How's it looking outside?"

The sound of static grated against his skull. "Sabre Command?"

More static.

Ferguson began to climb the stairs, the beams of light from his comrades flashed around above him. "Red Sabre One, you don't have much time. Get the principal and exfil through the underground tunnel. Sabre Command out."

As he caught up with the vanguard, Smudger asked, "What's the deal boss?"

Ferguson rushed past him, "Let's get a move on, lads. We don't have much time. Let's bag the principal, any other survivors that we find, and go back through the tunnel. Up top is compromised."

With an added urgency, the team took the remaining stairs two at a time, eventually coming to another door, held ajar by a shoe covered foot.

Spud motioned for quiet and knelt down. With his MP5 tucked behind him, his hands hovered over the smartly attired appendage. With the speed of a Champion SNAP! player, he grabbed hold of the ankle and pulled. He expected a degree of resistance, but none was forthcoming. Instead he fell backwards, clutching a foot which ended halfway up the shin. The sock was still pulled up as far as it could go, like a well-mannered school child.

"For fuck's sake," Spud cursed, and hurled the severed item into the corner of the landing. Retrieving his weapon, he pulled the door open and stood motionless by the doorway.

Ferguson drew level with the man and looked into the house. It reminded him of a village in Afghanistan they had cleared out. Having searched the other scorched buildings, they had come across a clothes shop, the only structure left that wasn't belching thick smoke.

They had kicked the door down and discovered where the villagers they had come to talk to were. Men, women and children were scattered around the room like spurned toys. The floor was slick with their blood. Ferguson remembered the obtuse angles the limbs were positioned at, as if the limits of their bendiness was being tested.

The scene within the entrance of number ten Downing Street was a few shades removed. The blood had soaked into the thick carpets, but the stench of death and murder was rife. At the bottom of the stairs, beneath a picture of a relaxed looking Winston Churchill, two police officers, still wearing their pointy helmets, were prying sticky fingers into the chest cavity of a suited young woman. Life had long since drained from her, and as they tugged at her innards her chest rose and fell as if she still breathed.

With fresh meat on offer, the two officers, their white shirts now a pinky-red hue, clambered to their feet. A piece of half chewed kidney rolled off the top of PC Eustace's body armour and hit the dead woman on the nose. The pair moaned at the intruders, seeking back up from their deceased brethren.

As they staggered towards them, Eustace bent over and vomited a stream of pulped meat and stringy sinew onto the ruined floor. Ferguson saw red. He pulled his weapon up to his shoulder and fired a round into each of the two coppers. They collapsed onto the floor, their duty, and supper, done.

He was stirred from his rage by the sound of pounding against a door. Ferguson stepped over the dead bodies and peered through the spyhole and into the world outside. A face, missing a cheek and showing exposed tombstones of ivory, blocked most of the picture outside. As it moved to one side, he saw that the horde was at least twenty deep.

Pulling away from the door, Ferguson ordered, "Spud, Denny, take the first floor. Me and Smudger are going for the Cabinet Room. That's where COBRA were meeting. We don't have much time, so get it done quickly." Without delay, Spud and Denny peeled off and headed towards the wide staircase, ensuring that the woman who was being feasted on had a bullet put through her skull.

With Ferguson in the lead, they headed down the corridor towards the Ante Room. More bodies in various states of dismemberment were strewn along the journey. Many were missing limbs, or their chest cavities exposed; clutches of organ lay scattered around them.

Not wishing to delay any longer, Ferguson got to the Ante Room door and kicked it in. It splintered and swung lazily to one side. Inside was another well-dressed man, tucking into an arm, still with a tattered sleeve wrapped around it. Wishing to make up for his earlier actions, Denny brushed past Ferguson and executed the zombie with a round to the back of its head.

Two doors were in front of them. Ferguson pointed to the left one, and on the count of three, barged his way into the room. At first the door resisted; the Captain saw that a makeshift barricade—an antique drinks cabinet—barred the way. "Hello?" he shouted, listening out for a reply. Hearing nothing, he pummelled the door with his boot, until a sufficient gap was made for him and Denny to enter.

The long oak table—which the pair were familiar with from television reports—was covered with paper and powered down laptops. "Hello?" Ferguson asked tersely, scanning the room, weapon ready. Chairs were overturned and the other exits were also buried behind piled up furniture. Denny tapped the Captain on the shoulder and pointed to someone the other side of the table.

Even from a few feet away, through the lens of his mask, he could see it was the Prime Minister. The well-coiffed hair was immaculate. He had his back to the two SAS men, and was kneeling on the ground, as if he was praying or mourning.

"Sir, we are here to get you out of here. We have to leave. *Now.*" Ferguson sidled round the table and stopped dead. The Prime Minister was straddling the legs of the Chancellor of the Exchequer, Oliver Bacon. Methodically the PM pushed podgy fingers into the guts of the dead man, pulled out chunks of red meat and shoved them in his mouth.

Ferguson's headset buzzed. "Red Sabre One, do you have eyes on the principal X-Ray?"

Letting his MP5 slide round his back, Ferguson thumbed the intercom. "Affirmative, Sabre Command, I have eyes on the principal." His other hand pulled out his pistol from its holster.

"Red Sabre One, are you able to extract him?"

Sensing a new supply of sustenance, the Prime Minister dropped the remains of the liver and began to stand up. With red stained hands reaching for the two men, he let out a low moan. Captain Ferguson raised his weapon. "Negative, Sabre Command, they're gone." He waited until the Prime Minister was a few feet away before firing into the dead man's forehead. "They're all gone."

# SENSELESS APPRENTICE

Screaming. They're always bloody screaming. I don't mind so much, except these days my senses aren't quite what they used to be, ya know? You'd think that right now, given my current predicament, pronounced hearing abilities would be a real boon, a good foundation to build on.

But no.

Turns out it's as much use as a phone box in a Trappist monastery. The screams sound like my head is strapped to an amp at a 'Nephilim of Doom' gig. It's all encompassing, and a tad on the annoying side.

Sure, the screaming and pleading never last long, before a hiss of air escapes as their throat opens up, or you nick an artery and it turns into a wet gurgling, gasping sound.

Such is life, or whatever the hell you call *this* now. Some things work a little better, most a lot worse. Before, *it*, well, I had perfect twenty-twenty vision. The optometrist, a South African chap, said I had 'perfect hunter gatherer vision'. Now, though, I'm lucky if I can see to the end of a safe house.

One definite plus point: the old sense of smell is not as good as it once was. That is a blessing. I'd estimate that one in three of them void their bowels once they go. It's disgusting. Bad enough when you're crouching there, all fingers and thumbs, rooting through the remains of their digestive tract, you know, the good bits, and you realise you're sat in a growing puddle of filth.

Animals, the bloody lot of them.

Tell ya what though. You certainly feel stronger. But the more I think about it—and that's one thing I get to do a lot of these days—whether that's some weird rigor mortis thing or a genuine supernatural power, I still haven't worked out. Pretty handy, though.

Was never the quickest, even less so since I got snagged. Have to say that getting the ole leg busted a few weeks back hasn't helped matters in the slightest.

Still see it once in a while. The bone. Think it's called the femur, sticking through the skin like a broken tent pole. Flaps of skin and muscle, a pure guess if I'm being honest. I'm no Doctor, but it looks like muscle should do, all dangling through the hole where my kneecap used to be.

You'd think it would've hurt. It probably did. I can't recall. But now, with every ridiculously slow step, even though I can hear the ends of the bone rubbing together like millstones, I don't even feel it.

The sound really does make my teeth grind, though.

Pretty much what I'm doing now actually as I just…yep, that's got it, right through the skin. Bit of tendon or something there, I think. Why do I always get the stringy ones? I do wonder if they were cooked a bit, would it help?

Yes, yes, I know, they're warm when you first get stuck in, and the cooling process takes a bit of time, but I do deliberate if they were, I dunno, grilled? Baked? Gently fried? Perhaps wrapped in foil, that stuff they give out after you've run a marathon, wrapped up in that, placed on a fire for fifteen minutes, poach them like salmon. Would that make them a bit more delectable?

Am I dribbling?

Ha, no, it's just a vein. I think. You find some dubious selections of meat around these parts, especially in the cities. This one bloke, WOW. Seriously, he was like eating a pork chop, except it was all rind. That got the old gag reflex going. That's weird, too.

So, I have no circulation, obviously. The hours I put in at the gym on my abs was completely wasted, as my muscle tone is disappearing faster than our food supplies.

No?

That's a zombie joke. My bad.

So yeah, lungs are about as much use as a voucher to learn the tango. My blood, at least the stuff which didn't leave me once *she* got hold of me, is left to congeal round my ankles and fingers.

Ha, not so much cankles, as blankles, you having that? No?

Tough crowd.

What was I saying? Ah yes, gag reflex. Hang on, let me just, urgh, must've been a smoker. Those adverts were right you know. There are some truly disgusting things growing inside the human body.

Anyway, back to the porker. Should've known it was a bad call to nibble on him, but it's not as if I have much choice, eh? Free will, like my eyesight, dating options and carefully constructed ten year career plan, has long since gone down the Swannee.

I was stumbling after Mister Chewy, hey, it's a difficult thing to do when one of your legs bends in two places. It takes a degree of skill, which…well, I don't possess anymore. I'm just trying to make the best out of a bad situation these days, okay?

The guy saw me and bolted, as much as he was able to. It may sound a little mean, but *waddle* is a more than suitable adjective for what I saw him do. Hell, ole one-arm-flat-cap-zombie moved faster than he did. He brought him down actually. I get there, eventually. Luckily he's not screaming; more a gentle mewling, just like a little kitten, aww.

The best bits are already bagsied. Someone is sticking their broken fingernails into his eye socket. You know where you stand with the eyes, can't really get a bad one. I kneel down, as best as a man can with one mashed up leg, and I'm by the small of his back. I pull his shirt up way easier than I ever managed to with any of my lady friends. I'm in the zone; I guess impulse and instinct has some uses eh?

I manage to dig my fingers through his skin and start clawing away. Knew there and then that we'd got a bad 'un. Started shoving fistfuls of what I thought was meat into my mouth…

I'm chewing and I'm chewing and I'm chewing, and it's still there, it just won't break down. The chunk slides to the side of my mouth. Better teeth over there you see, they're the grinders, yeah?

So, I grind and I grind, and nothing. What's left of my brain obviously thinks that all is good and tried to swallow it. Not as if I'm going to choke to death, eh? It hit the back of my throat before it came back up again. Couldn't believe it. I've had more warm dinners since I turned than, well, a lot of 'em, but he's the only one I've rejected.

Think it was a unanimous thing, as the others, like me, late to the gig, weren't that fussed either. The soft stuff went down okay, just urgh, lesson learned.

Except *you* don't learn any lessons these days, not any that you can put into practise. Case in point, I've not long started to tuck into this one, and I'm done. For reasons unknown to me, I'm up again and ambling down the road. Unbelievable. It makes no sense. Logic is not the friend of the undead, or whatever the hell I am now.

Looks like…yep, heading over to that door over there. I can hear the moaning of my kin. Took a while for me to work out which moan meant what. Sure *he* gets it, part of their nature I guess, but me, well, I'm still thinking of things on the corporeal breathing plane. I know enough to have a decent idea what my next port of call is though, that's enough for me.

And here we go again, another boarded up house, another locked bloody door, and what do I do? Hang on, three-two-one, there we go, bang, bang, bang on the bloody door.

Stupid isn't it?

I can learn the different moans and their meaning. Okay, there aren't many, but *he* can't quite grasp the premise of open and closed. Does my head in, which I've been thinking lately, wouldn't actually be that bad a thing, I don't reckon.

Honest.

Look at it from my point of view, this vessel of mine doesn't sleep, so all that good stuff that happened when I used to fall asleep—ya know; dreams, white blood cell production, morning glory—all gone. All I get is a constant stream of screaming, blurry images and moaning.

I can still remember my last dream. I was back at my old school. It was knocked down years ago, but I was having a mooch around as it once was. It had aged and the people I used to know were playing football or beating the crap out of Matty.

Got woken up by a banging not too dissimilar to what I'm doing now, I suppose. Everyone panicked. This was back in the early days. Before anyone could say 'who the bloody hell is that at the door?' a horde of them got in and started tucking in.

They were proper lucky bastards that day. I wager that door must've had a crap lock on it. This one is a proper Yale lock, I think, and still I go, bang, bang, bang. I sound like a decent percussionist, but it'll take a miracle to—

WOAH.

Why the hell did she open up? Mad look in her eyes, that one. Snuck right past me. Not difficult, I know.

I do have the reflexes of a three wheeled rusty roller skate.

In a puddle.

At night.

You get the picture. Anyway, the game is afoot, heh heh heh, let's see what's in here then.

That annoys me too. The lack of control over direction, even with my crappy eyesight, I can see that the doorway on the right over there is open, but what does *he* do? Yep, try to go up the stairs.

In my state.

With my leg.

I despair, I really do. This could take a while, gives me a chance to have a bit of a ponder.

Can still remember the one that got me; this petite little blonde. I'd only seen two zombies in the flesh, so to speak. They were proper mashed up. One was lying on the bonnet of a car having been launched through the windscreen. Shards of glass as big as your arm were sticking out of places you don't want arm length shards of glass sticking out of.

The other fella is all smashed up like an accordion against the dashboard. Both of them were waving their hands at me, as if to reel me in closer. Idiots. There was no way I was gonna fall for that one, especially given how messed up they were.

Remember kids, always wear your seatbelts.

So between those two and the odd film I'd seen, my view on zombies was that they were pretty awful to look at. Not her, though. She was stunning.

Okay, so yes, she had a slight…tinge to her skin, and if you're being pedantic, one of her ears had been chewed off, but I didn't find that out till later.

I thought she was one of the survivors I hadn't met yet. Thought my luck was in at last. Our little sanctuary had been breached and this little stunner had come to me, to be her white knight.

I'd carry her off on the back of a mighty stallion, towards a horizon framed by the setting sun, to a cottage with fresh crisp bed linen and chilled champagne.

No.

Aside from the lack of equine transportation, and the fact that with all the fires the only chance you'd get to see the sunset would be if you were on the International Space Station. She wasn't there for my understated looks; she was there to sink her teeth into my neck.

It was while I was being shaken, like a ragdoll in the mouth of a strangely erotic dead woman, that I finally saw the missing ear. As I felt the growth in my pants subside and my collar get wetter and warmer, I had but one thought run across my mind.

Why me?

Oh, hang on, here we go, finally made it to the top of the stairs. Man alive, think the bone is sticking out more now in my leg. I'm all lopsided.

Wait a moment, what the hell was that?

Pretty sure something just bounced off my head.

No you idiot, look the other side.

Seriously, this gets irritating fast.

Over there.

No. There.

And another one. Yep, right in the nose, from that cracking sound, I'm going to make an educated guess that my dead nose is now broken.

Yep, there it is.

Broken nose confirmed.

I can see the tip pointing to the left. Well isn't that just bloody marvellous.

Okay. That was definitely another direct hit. At this rate, I'm going to have no nose.

How do I smell?

Terrible.

Oh, you've heard it?

Over there dummy. Honestly, it's at times like this I wish I had some kind of remote control, rather than being nothing more than a voyeur. Finally. What is that?

Ahhh, it's a brick! Should've realised really, especially the way my head has been rocked backwards throughout the bombardment. You get annoyed very quickly with those who are left alive. Not sure if it's jealousy that they lasted longer, but their futile resistance gets right on your tits.

Even more so when they lob chunks of masonry at your noggin.

WOAH, steady on tiger! You'll take someone's eye out with that bloody huge knife. Oh, it's my eye you're trying to take out. Well, give it a go, not as if it's doing dumbass here any favours. Perhaps losing one might make *him* more careful in future.

Here I go, going to try and grab him and—

Bollocks.

I know for a fact that fingers don't grow back, not even when I was alive. Hang about, go on mate, get him, go on…

Huzzah!

That'll teach him. Too focused on me, weren't you? Yeah, and you didn't see my dead mate here sneaking up behind you, did you? No, you didn't. Look at you now, snivelling away, and…yep, the screaming begins.

Again.

It's enough to drive you mad. Given the circumstances it undoubtedly happened a while ago. Probably helps to explain why I'm talking to some figment of my imagination.

Are you real?

Oh, hang on, here we go. The laborious process of kneeling and…yep, dig those remaining digits in, dig them in good. Grab hold of that rib. Go on. You've got a decent sized hole there, just reach in and give it a bit of a tug.

Okay, a bit more of a tug.

Yank it.

For Pete's sake, PULL HIS BLOODY RIBS OU—

Yay! Finally. Ha, not so stabby now are you? No you're not. It's time to tuck in and see what you're like. Hmm, not too bad, non-smoker, worked out a bit, too many tattoos, in my opinion, but…oh no, that's just the blood.

Man, there is a lot, wooooooo, flashback time…that blonde girl trying to rip out my jugular, my shirt soaking up all the blood. Knew it wasn't going to end well.

I'd passed out, or so I thought. Always reckoned that there would be a tunnel.

And light.

Loads of reports of tunnels of light, if I'm remembering correctly.

None of that.

I'd say it was more like being drunk and then waking up on the living room floor of your crappy one bedroom flat. You know how your eyes are all squinty and blurry? Got a headache like a bastard, tongue and mouth as dry as Gandhi's flip-flop, and the pièce de résistance, lying down in a puddle of vomit.

So swap the bile for your own blood and that's a pretty close approximation.

Another point to note. First off, you think you're in control. The body that you think is your own is quite happily doing the checkpoint you do.

Ooohhh my neck is wet—puts hand to neck.

Ooohhh, my eyes are all blurry—rub eyes.

So far, so good. Then in your mind, you think, 'Well that was lucky. Let's get up and get out of here before one of those zombies comes back and finishes me off.'

Nothing.

Hmmm, must still be drunk. Let's try sending that electrical impulse across that synapse again. Up we go.

Nothing.

I don't know Latin, so I made up something, 'Standus Uppus'.

Nothing.

I also noticed for the first time since *it*, that no words were coming out. I was chatting away solely via the medium of internal monologue. The sound of the vocal cords doing their usual job was noticeably absent. As my mind wandered, I said 'echo, echo, echo' in my head, just to test the acoustics. As if by magic, I stood up.

Now we're cooking on gas. Pretty sure all that's happened is some kind of brain embolism.

No biggie.

Nothing which can't be fixed.

A few days ago when the modern world, and its assortment of medicine, actually existed of course.

That thought didn't occur until later.

Hang on, never seen that before. What is it? Human anatomy was never a strong point of mine. Another thing I'm learning as I go along. Lungs are like faces, I've found out; no two pairs look the same. The first time I saw some as I, sorry, *he*, hauled them out of their home, I thought they were kidneys.

True story.

Nope, still none the wiser, I'll let him carry on, nothing to see here. Not that I have a choice about what I can see anyway. No sleep. I know I've mentioned that already, but it's worth saying again. No blinking, no flirtatious winks, nothing. Twenty four-seven, until I decompose or someone mashes my brain up, I'll be watching.

Bit like that song by Sting.

Right, back to the ole origin story.

So up I got, the room was pretty dark, could hear some slurping beneath me and some shuffling out in the hallway. Then, out of the gloom, I saw her, standing there, without a care in the world. Miss bloody blonde Chomper. Ambling around like she owned the place, blood all over her chin.

That's *my* blood, you harlot! That's supposed to be inside me, being pumped around!

You know?

In use.

By me.

Not dripping onto your rather smashing blouse.

Despite my British sensibilities, I was determined to remonstrate with her. This kind of vicious, unprovoked assault cannot be tolerated, not without some kind of sternly worded riposte. With a vicious, barbed put-down formed in my brain, I go to speak.

. . .

And again, nothing comes out. Just the words in my head.

Hey, I'm not even looking at her now; I'm wandering off towards the kitchen. Turn around.

Eh?

Turn around.

I COMMAND YOU.

Nothing.

This is ridiculous. I'm pretty sure I mastered the art of movement at a very early age. It quickly became one of those things I did without thinking. I was pretty good at it, from what I remember.

I'm there, dragging my feet down the hallway, and I can't do anything about it. I can't speak, I can't move, let me just…nope, I can't even slap myself in the face to see if it's all a dream.

It was a bit of a pickle, I tell ya.

Hello, back to the present. Here we go. *He* always gets bored pretty quick, wonder if it's worth the effort sometimes. Go through all this hassle of bringing them down, and then after a few lazy bites and half-hearted attempts at pulling out their intestines, up I get and we're onto the next thing. Oh, there's another feeding moan nearby, sounds muffled, I bet you a fiver it's behind that door over there.

The middle one.

Bet you.

Yes, yes, I know that technically I owe you one hundred and fifteen pounds, but I'm confident this time.

The middle one.

Tell ya what? I'm that confident, let's make it twenty.

What's the matter, are you chicken?

Typical, naturally, should you present *him* with three doors, he stumbles over his crappy leg and head-butts the wall.

Great, it won't sort the nose out you know?

So, here we go, what's behind door number one? Well, it's not locked. That's a decent start for my chance to reduce the arrears.

It's…the airing cupboard.

YES. I can practically smell the reduction of my virtual IOU.

Sod it, let's make it thirty. I'm good for it.

You know I am! Where am I going to go? Hmm?

Okay, door number two, or the payday door as I'm going to call it. Unlocked, not great. Hang on though, what's this? The door is stuck.

Nice one, dummy.

Great, yes! Let's go and bang on it again, eh?

Honestly, the apes from 2001 had more about them than the undead.

This could take a while.

So, going back to that hallway, in the days of yore. Something caught my eye as I'm trudging down the squelchy carpet. My head turns—without me instructing it to do so, I'd like to add—and there I am.

I do not look well, I'm going to admit that.

Not well at all.

It did help to explain why the world looked a little jauntily angled. Ole Blondie must've torn through the throat muscle, and tendons, as my head is on a bit of a tilt.

That was annoying first off; took me ages to get over that, but it wasn't as if I could feel it.

So when you think about it, I've actually saved hundreds of pounds on chiropractor bills. Got to find the silver lining wherever you can these days, especially when you're faced with the very real notion that you've shuffled off this mortal coil.

I think I was more miffed about my shirt being utterly ruined.

If you don't deal with blood stains quickly, you have no chance whatsoever. Like some kind of old time comedy act, my hands start patting the mirror. This moan comes out of me without so much as a thought. Another few pats and I'm off down the corridor again.

That's when I knew that something was amiss.

Oh hello.

Finally, the banging has prevailed. Think I've lost another finger in the process. Must've been hanging on by a thread of what passes for my skin nowadays. Well played you idiot, down to just the thumb and my lonesome pinky on the right hand now. That was my favourite hand as well. There better be something worthwhile in here.

Hmmm, I can hear something, but it doesn't sound very moany. Well, that body without a head lying there would explain why the door was a little tough to open. Big ole blighter he was too. Wait a bet-winning moment, there's something over there…in the corner.

Oh bugger.

It's a dog.

A bloody dog.

Nice one, thanks champ.

Yes, yes, that's another thirty I owe you.

I hope I rot quickly, otherwise I'm going to be in some serious imaginary debt.

No point growling at me, you mutt. I don't like this either, you know. I wish I was anywhere but here, perhaps having a cheeky afternoon pint in the boozer.

What time is it anyway?

Semantics. I'd rather be in the pub and you'd probably prefer to be chasing after a stick in the park. Well, I'm off again anyway.

Animals aren't really part of the diet. Must be the fur, I reckon. *He's* not even so much as made an effort to have a bit of a nibble on any we've come across. And no, before you ask, it isn't because of my reduced foot speed.

Pretty sure that's some kind of discrimination by you then.

Yes, maybe I am a little mad with you now.

I've still got feelings you know. Sure, I can't show them at all, due to my face being a little bereft of emotional reflection. If you cut me, do I not bleed? Okay, bad example, that ain't gonna happen.

I've lost where I was. Oh yeah! Animals. Cats just outright avoid us. You hear the hiss but it's rare you see them these days. Dogs, though, well they go one of two ways. They can whimper and ignore you, bolting off as soon as they can, or…

Great.

Yes, or else they turn into Cujo, like this little tinker. I've seen a pack of Cockapoos take down a zombie before. They ripped the poor sod limb from limb.

This is not going to end well.

Naturally, *he* is off, that moaning is still pulling us in. Going to be door number three eh?

I can still hear that dog growling behind me. Why am I not moving anymore? Ah, now I look down.

Give me strength!

You know what? When the sun came up this morning I had two hands working fine, each with their full complement of digits, and now…yep, I'm free of his jaws, which is good, but am now missing an entire hand. See, the skin doesn't have the same tensile strength as before. You'd think it would go all hard and be like armour.

Nope, goes all sallow and tears really easily. You learn the hard way that there is just no suitable after-death skin care routine. I lost this patch of skin on my elbow a few days back when it got caught on a door latch.

Numb-nuts here didn't care.

Even when I'm snagged on it, his first thought isn't to gently tease the affected area off the impediment.

Nope.

He adopts the 'keep on walking and see what happens' approach.

Got peeled like an onion.

Well at least Mister Dog is happy playing with my hand. Might stop him coming back for seconds, or worse, getting hold of the bone sticking through my leg.

Door number three. Okay, so the moaning has got louder. Yes, fine, have some more imaginary currency. Remember that I will be winning that back. Just been on a bit of a bad run recently, that's all.

Ahh, there we go. Mind you, with the amount of walking dead in there already, I doubt we'll get anything decent. Yep, even *he* isn't bothered, off on a general meander now then.

I hate all this downtime.

I bore too easily you see. Never a problem back in the day when I was breathing and all that jazz. Now though, it is really irritating.

I suppose I do sound quite whingy, but look at my situation.

For one, I'm dead, and have been for…erm…a while now, must be months. Difficult to tell, not as if we record any of this in a diary. That would be dull; staggered around, ate a few people, banged on another door for a bit, made my leg worse, missed getting my head stoved in by pure chance.

Day after day after day. The same bloody thing.

I can't feel or sense what *he* thinks either, so I doubt he can listen to me and my idle prattling. Probably for the best. Don't really want my negativity to detract from what *he* has to do.

One thing's for sure, I couldn't do it.

No siree Bob.

If I had any control over my functions, like I used to…urgh, makes me shudder thinking about it.

Okay, so it was an imaginary shudder.

You can be such a pedant at times.

So, I'm dead in body, but still alive somewhere in my brain. Must be the same for all the others. Don't know for sure, but I would put money on it.

No, not a bet, not as if me or you can prove it one way or the other, is it?

I do look at them when I get the opportunity. Try to see if I can see any hint of internal conflict, any glimmer of someone else living behind their dead eyes.

Thought I saw something once, but it turned out to be a nest of maggots which burst out.

That was gross.

I've seen some pretty disgusting things since that girl ripped my throat out, but that is definitely in the top three.

Another hazard of being dead; nothing respects your authority any more. You're top of the food tree in one sense, yet at the bottom in others.

It's swings and roundabouts.

A real mixed bag, as my nan used to say.

So I guess I'll just go on. Until one of the living manages to reduce my decaying brain into mulch, or I literally fall apart.

How long does it take for a body to decompose? Number of factors, I guess; environmental conditions, light, state of skin on reanimation, whether your designated driver is a bit more careful and doesn't let bits of you get peeled off by inanimate objects.

That's annoyed me, that has.

Losing the hand was a pain in the arse, definitely, but I could've got out of that situation with a lot more than I did.

Just a general lack of care and attention, that's all.

Well, looks like upstairs is all cleared out. Not a bad haul, but we've had better.

That supermarket was still the best one.

Not that I'm counting.

I do find it abhorrent, but you can't help but take a partial interest.

It isn't as if I can go off and watch TV is it?

Great, staircases, bad enough to deal with going up, let alone when you need to go down-
Bloody hell!

Nice one you absolute monger! Just ruddy typical that you miss the first step out and end up in a heap at the bottom.

Is that?

Yes.

Today is really starting to get on my nerves now.

That's the leg gone too, then.

Give me strength…

So, let's summarise. In the space of, what, ten minutes I lost some fingers to a knife…okay, to a machete-wielding maniac.

Then another finger goes following *his* best Ringo impression on the door.

Our canine friend then takes one hand.

Finally, to cap it all off, I've fallen down the stairs and lost a leg.

Don't try to stand up!

Seriously, it just…no…it's not—
YOU CAN'T PUT ANY WEIGHT ON IT.
I'm now going to spend the rest of my existence crawling around like those other poor sods. You can kiss goodbye to getting anything decent to eat any more.
Nope, all gone now.
We're going to end up with the leftovers.
The bits that no-one wants.
Ah well, it doesn't matter I suppose. Just as long as it's you and me.
Forever.
Till undeath us do part.
You won't leave me, will you?
Good, knew you wouldn't.
Okay, let's make things a bit more interesting, I bet you a tenner that dumbass here tries to stand up again.
You in?

DEAD DROP

CHAPTER ONE

"You've never peeked inside one? Not even once?" Turner pushed herself back from the desk. The rusty castor wheels squeaked in resistance.

Ceepher, still in the act of counting the red elastic bands, didn't even look across. "Nope, never. In these days, your word has to count for something."

Turner looked outside at the sprawling camp; dishevelled people trudged along the wooden walkways. Some of the new arrivals would stumble on the sections which bowed into muddy puddles, looking around quickly to see if anyone had seen them. Even after everything, people still had their vanity to preserve.

"I'm five short," Ceepher stated, holding out the palm of his hand. "I had to take care of a family of four, picking that up for you. The least you can do is make sure you pay me the agreed amount."

Turner smirked. "Nothing gets past you, huh?" She plunged her hand into a hidden jacket pocket and pulled out a large ball, constructed from wound around red elastic bands. "Were they fresh? The family?"

Ceepher looked down at his hands, which were coated in grime and splatters of black congealed blood. "They'd been there since Day of the Zed, by the smell of them. Don't see many new ones these days. The stupid died first, remember? Guessing hell is still full."

Turner placed ten bands on Ceepher's palm and closed it up into a fist. "There's a few extra, for the ferryman." He nodded back a thanks. "Say, you wanna see inside?"

Lingering by the desk was the sole acknowledgement Turner received, who smirked and pulled out a knife from a sheath on her belt. Placing the blade under the twine, she pinged the bond free with two deft flicks. She went to open the box, before noticing Ceepher was looking on intently. "Be my guest." She pushed the package across to the courier.

After two-and-a-half years of running jobs, and sticking to his one tenet, it took Ceepher a few seconds before he stirred from his reverie, and dared to even touch the cardboard box. With the camp commandant looking on, Ceepher peeled open the flaps, revealing a sea of foam packing quavers.

"Those things get everywhere," Turner whinged. "Go on. I'll get one of the guards to clear it up after." Placing one hand on the opening, Ceepher carefully tipped the box upside down, scattering the packing material over the desk and cascading onto the floor. It seemed to go on forever, some kind of TARDIS containing a never-ending foam waterfall.

As the last dregs silently fell from their cardboard prison, Ceepher slid his hand into the box. Turner smiled as she saw a look of bemusement manifest on the deliveryman's face. Realising what it was, he pulled out a polished skull and set it down on the table, atop a pristine blotter board. "There's enough skulls out there already, you know? Why the hell do you want one picked, packed and delivered?"

Turner picked at the skull as if she were carrion, plucking one of the foam quavers from the eye socket and discarding it on the floor. "This is a cast of Elvis Presley's head."

Ceepher shrugged. "And? What use is that? Not sure you've noticed these days, but beyond that wall is death and shit. Perhaps if you got out of that chair once in a while, you w—"

"Don't lecture me! Who set up this gated community? You? From what I heard, you were too busy drinking yourself into a coma every night for the first few months when the dead started walking. Whilst you were speaking to God down the porcelain telephone each day, *some* of us were out there fighting, trying to take the world back. My freedom, and everyone else's behind these walls, has been bought and paid for in blood, mine included."

Bristling, Ceepher clenched his fists together. "You know nothing about what happened, it wa—"

Turner held a hand up, stopping him in mid-flow. "No, I don't, not fully, but by the same turn, you know nothing of me."

The pair stared at each other, the air between them crackled with energy. Finally, Ceepher acquiesced. "Fine…just think there are more worthwhile things to be trying to get these days, not…trinkets like this." He tapped the crown of the skull with dirty fingernails.

Swivelling on her chair, Turner wheeled over to a three-quarter-high cabinet. Pulling on a pitted silver chain, which ended in her waistcoat pocket, she produced a small key. Holding it up for effect, she unlocked the cabinet and opened the doors. As she did, the opening strains to 'In The Ghetto', started up. "Appropriate. Wouldn't you agree?"

As Turner wheeled backwards, Ceepher peered across the room into the cabinet. Lined with crushed purple velvet, it was awash with pictures and personal effects of 'The King'.

Vinyl in dog-eared card sleeves were lined up at the bottom, below a turntable which spun idly around. Dead centre, there was a circular plinth. A small golden plaque, engraved with 'Elvis Aaron Presley' was screwed onto the front. With the reverence of a funeral director, Turner took the skull from the desk and placed it atop the squat pedestal.

Vacant eye sockets looked out into the room; Turner smiled and fiddled with the display until she was happy with its arrangement. "There, what do you think?"

"It's…a little creepy. What is that on the top shelf? By the comb, with the…is that hair?"

Turner nodded. Rubbing her hands on her trousers, she lifted the comb out gently, holding it up to the light from the window. "Taken from Graceland right after his death, you know. This arrived the day before the world went to pot. As for these…" Setting the comb back in its place, she placed a number of small ivory coloured chips on the palm of her hand and held it out.

Unsure at first, Ceepher sighed and walked towards the proffered hand. He picked one of the items up and studied it. A flash of realisation washed over him, and he dropped it back in Turner's hand. "Fingernails?"

Laughing, Turner brushed the brown shards back onto the shelf. Making sure everything was as it should be, she closed the cabinet up, locked it, and returned the key to her pocket. "Toenails, to be precise. One of the emergency responders who turned up to peel him off the toilet found them in the plughole."

Ceepher scratched at the palm of his hands. "You paid money for those?"

"Of course. They were quite a pretty penny."

"You're weird…"

Turner pulled herself back under her desk. "You call me weird? You're the one still wandering around out there, delivering god knows what to people. Why do it? Everyone who possesses a shred of sanity lives in a community like this one these days. There are only raiders, lunatics and the dead living beyond those walls. Why not take up a normal job and be done with it?"

Ceepher shoved the elastic bands into his jacket pocket, zipped it up, and nodded a thanks. He headed to the door. As he pulled it open, a doleful moan was carried aloft on the late afternoon breeze, over the breeze block wall, topped with a hedge of barbed wire. He turned back to the woman. "That life is not for me. It's best I'm not round people for too long, not any more. My life is out there, with the nutjobs. It's all I have these days."

"It won't bring them back," Turner said.

He tapped the door. "Maybe, but at least I can't see their dead faces in the boughs of trees, or burned out cars. If I lived here, I'd probably top myself or go postal. Perhaps even both. Given time."

"Each to their own," Turner conceded.

"Be seeing you, Jo," Ceepher said, stepping out onto the grubby welcome mat outside the mobile home.

Turner called out after him, "There's a man in the bar, says he has a job for someone stupid enough to take it. Said I know just the crazy bastard to do it. His name's Kipworth. You'll know him when you see him. Trust me."

Ceepher looked back and inclined his head. "Appreciate it."

"Take care of yourself out there, Ceepher. There will always be a place here waiting for you. When you're ready."

Closing the door behind him, Ceepher retrieved a cloth cap from an inner pocket, pulled it down his head, and headed for the bar.

CHAPTER TWO

The pub in the Melksham safe zone was imaginatively titled, 'Moonrakers', after the county's famous moniker for its residents.

Four separate mobile homes had been lashed together with plywood, sweat and crossed fingers, to form a social hub for the community. With garish floral carpet, salvaged from a number of local hostelries—chosen to keep the spirit of the English countryside public house alive—it was often bustling in the evening after the work of the day was done.

Ceepher trudged through the mud, each step a slurp and a squelch, the ground seeking to claim him to its boggy depths. Having watched numerous people come a cropper on the wooden duckboards, he decided to forgo civility and yomp directly through the quagmire to the pub.

A bouncer, dressed in a mud flecked black suit, idly swung a cricket bat, which had nine inch nails driven through the toe of the weapon. As Ceepher got closer, the man grinned and began to open the door in preparation.

"Good to see you again, my man. How you been keeping?" the guard asked.

Ceepher peeled the sweat-drenched cap from his head; traversing the gloop had been hard work. He scrunched it up and stuffed it into his pocket. "Not too bad cheers, Kristof. How's the wife and kids?"

Kristof tapped his fingers to his head in a mock salute. "Still out getting milk and the Sunday papers. Yours?"

"Still trying to find a parking spot, Kris."

With their standard pleasantries exchanged, Ceepher ducked under the lintel and into the bar. He kicked his boots against a metal umbrella stand, trying to remove some of the clod which hung from them, like some kind of oozing deformity. Realising it was a losing task, he gave up and headed to the bar, which ran three quarters the length of the four housing units.

"What'll it be?" the barman asked, his hand wrapped in a towel, which squeaked against the innards of a glass tankard.

Ceepher dusted off the top of a bar stool, checked it for any major wobbling, and plonked himself down. "Dare I ask what you have in?"

Spitting another wad of phlegm into the glass, the barman scrubbed away at some piece of detritus unseen. "We've just had some new scrumpy delivered. There's the latest batch of Farmer Coombes homebrew, or the local sloe gin. Pick a poison, friend."

"I'll have some of the Farmer Coombes, cheers. Sounds like the least lethal of the lot."

The barman grinned, revealing pegs of blackened teeth, each bordered its sibling with a thin division of plaque. "Choice of champions, friend." Yanking his hand from the glass, he set it on the bar in front of Ceepher before rooting around behind the bar. Retrieving a demijohn bottle, he pulled out the rubber stopper and went to pour.

"What are you doing?" Ceepher asked, covering the pint glass with his hand.

Puzzled, the barman looked from Ceepher's hand to his face, then to the glass, before repeating the process. After a few more circuits, and with a furrowed brow, he asked, "What's the matter friend? You changed your mind?"

Ceepher picked up the glass and held it in front of the barman's face. "You're new here huh? I'd like a glass that you haven't gobbed in, if it's not too much trouble. It may be the end of the world, but I don't really want to taste what you had for breakfast."

The barman began to laugh. "Why, of course, your lordship. Excuse me while I go and fetch the finest pewter tankard that we have. 'Ere mate, look around this place. Do you think that any of these glasses have been cleaned in a different way?"

Turning on his seat, Ceepher took in the clientele, most of whom huddled together in small groups, whispering amongst themselves. They cradled their glasses of booze as if it were their only remaining possession. He looked back to the barman, who had a finger plugged into his nostril, rummaging around for hidden gold. "Fine," Ceepher said, "but do me a favour and let me pour it."

Bowing, the barman passed the chunky glass container across the divide and resumed his nasal excavation, taking time to study his findings. Having filled the glass to the brim, Ceepher placed the booze back on the bar and slapped an elastic band onto the counter. "Much obliged to you," the barman said.

Daring a swig, Ceepher was pleasantly surprised that the hoppy Farmer Coombes was rather agreeable. Sure, it wasn't going to win any real ale awards, but the warm feeling in his guts, which was slowly spreading to his face, at least comforted him that it would do the job. Taking a moment to survey the bar, he spotted a man sitting in a corner booth, supping on a pint. Ceepher smirked, and made his way over.

"Kipworth, I presume?"

The man, who was staring intently into the cloudy contents of his drink, flashed Ceepher a look, before dipping a finger into his pint and prodding something within. As he pulled his finger out, the skin hissed and fizzed, "And you are?"

"Turner said you had a job for me…"

Having wiped his finger on a pair of meticulously pressed trousers, the man pushed his glasses back up the bridge of his nose and peered at the dishevelled man in front of him. "My good man, how do you know who I am?"

Ceepher stood back and waved an arm at the denizens of Moonrakers. "Take a look around at the alternatives. You're the only one here who isn't covered in shit."

"Quite," Kipworth replied dryly.

Gesturing to the empty seat, the suited man nodded, and Ceepher took his place.

Kipworth resumed the autopsy of his beverage. "There's something in here…just can't quite see what it is."

"Knowing this place, and the likely production methods of that scrumpy you're drinking, I'd say it's probably a good job you don't find out. What you don't know can't hurt ya."

This made Kipworth look up. "Which is something I believe you are familiar with, hmm? Ms Turner told me that she knew a courier who was…*discreet*. In these troubled times, that, along with a man's word, are two commodities in short supply."

Ceepher took a big gulp from his drink and wiped his mouth with his sleeve. The ale had developed an interesting aftertaste of watercress. "It's a lot easier in my profession to not concern yourself with what you're carrying. As long as it's not too heavy, and I get paid when I'm told I will, there's no problem. Speaking of which…"

With a fingernail hooked in the foreign object, Kipworth looked up. "Ah yes, of course, fiscal compensation. I see you are a man who wants to get straight to the point. I can respect that. Payment is three hundred bands, one hundred up front, the rest upon delivery."

Halfway through taking a sip, Ceepher held the glass to his lips. Finally he asked, "Three hundred? You better not be jerking me around pal."

Kipworth cursed as he lost the tenuous grip on the cider's lurking item. "I too am a man of my word, Mister Ceepher. I have no intention of…jerking you around, as you so eloquently state."

"Okay, so where and when?"

Pulling out a pair of spotless leather gloves from his jacket pocket, Kipworth faced Ceepher. "Tomorrow morning, by the front gates. I'll be waiting at seven o'clock sharp. You need to get the package to the Bishopdown Farm settlement within forty eight hours, no later. Else the remainder of your payment is forfeit."

Ceepher scowled, "Salisbury? That place is a fucking tomb from what I've heard. In that time frame, I'd have to go right through the city centre."

Stretching out each finger in his gloves, Kipworth sighed. "Those are my terms. Take them, or leave them. I'm sure I can find someone else who could make this delivery instead."

The near empty glass hit the table with a thud. "I never said it was impossible, just that it would be tricky. Fine. You're on, Kipworth. Just one thing…"

"Yes?"

Ceepher shoved his hand into Kipworth's drink and pulled out a rotting rat's skull. Its eyes had dissolved away, and the fur was lank. Placing it in front of the smartly dressed man, he said in a low voice, "Make sure you don't stiff me on the payment, else you and this little fella will have one thing in common. Are we clear?"

Stifling upchuck, Kipworth placed a gloved hand over his lips, nodded and mumbled, "Crystal."

"Good, I'll see you in the morning. Make sure you have my upfront payment ready. I want to make the most of the daylight hours, before the biters get even more bitey."

Ceepher finished his drink, slapped Kipworth on the shoulder and headed back to the bar.

CHAPTER THREE

As the sun crawled up over the horizon, coruscating bands of orange and red lit up the clouds like a net of balloons held in reserve for a surprise party. Ceepher's boots clumped on the road as he picked his way through a mass of snarled up cars.

Having spent over two years traversing the countryside, now bereft of transportation save a few bicycles, Ceepher had arrived at the conclusion that the safest way was by walking the roads. Early on, and with a tight deadline to make, he had tried to pick his way through Savernake forest in mid-autumn. With the light fading, and fat drops of rain hitting the yellowing canopy around him, he was robbed of the advantage of both sight and sound.

After the fifth time of being ambushed by a group of the undead, he swore from that moment on he'd stick to the roads. Even with nature reclaiming the world as its own once more, with trees, weeds and vines blooming and covering everything man had made, the tarmac roads prevailed.

The main advantage was that you could see for miles, handy to spot the oblivious shambling corpses, or even rarer, human survivors. Ceepher smiled, Turner was right about one thing: the sane ones were behind the walls now; only madmen chose to live in this cesspit.

He cast another glance at the map; about thirty miles he guessed, a touch more given that the safe zone he was heading for was on the far side of Salisbury. The mere mention of the place tightened a knot of grief in his guts, wringing his guilt and plucking on his sorrow. He thought back to the beginning, when this all started.

Everyone, himself included, was so cocksure that it would be over quickly. Especially being in Salisbury, and with the army barracks nearby. Heavily armed soldiers had been deployed in and around the city within days of the government confirming what the media had been reporting on for days.

Though he was used to it now, the headline, 'THE DEAD WALK', was still imprinted in his brain. With promises made by Generals, chests swollen with medals and ribbons, Ceepher was sure that in a few days things would return to normal.

However, the army were trained to fight a conventional foe, and the tide of shuffling corpses were like no enemy they had ever faced before. Bullets were poured into their rotting masses, yet destroyed so few of their number. They had been taught to aim for the centre mass, not the head and brain, the shots which were necessary to send them back to whatever hell that had spawned them.

By the time they had realised their folly, the dead had broken through the lines. Soldiers screamed as broken fingernails tore through their skin, peeled their flesh from bones and scooped still steaming organs from their cavities.

Once they had feasted on the city's defenders, they turned their attention to the populace, now nothing more than fish in a barrel. The horde worked their way through the streets like a virus. Mobs of zombies tore down makeshift barricades and battered down doors. Amongst those people trapped inside, surrounded, some made their peace and gave themselves willingly, whilst others resisted. The pitiful few that survived the onslaught were forever changed.

Ceepher was counted amongst them.

Working his way past the last rusting car, he dared to look inside. A desiccated skeleton, clutching a bundle of rags and bones to its bosom, looked out accusingly with empty sockets.

I didn't damn you to your fate.

Though he knew those words were true in this case, he could not persuade himself of their virtue to the past. He used to joke with Emma, his wife, about the list of DIY tasks he had promised to get done, yet made no inroads into.

"Next weekend for sure."

"Can't this weekend. I'm knackered after work."

"Just need to get some different screws."

"Don't worry, I'll get the ladder for the loft. Not like it's urgent."

Ceepher remembered how they thought they had all the time in the world to get into the attic. Only after he had managed to pull himself up into the roof space, able to look down at his wife and daughter, did he realise that his optimism had been misplaced. He witnessed first-hand how their desperation increased in sync with the volume of the infected outside their house, thrashing around, trying to get in.

"How are we going to get up there?"

"It's too high. Come back down, we'll find another way."

"I can hear them…they're going to get in."

"Just take Boo. Leave me here."

With one hand holding onto the rim of the open loft hatch, he had reached down with the other for little Kerry. Emma had picked her up and passed her to him, and he'd held onto her arm as if it was the only thing anchoring him to reality.

Then the dead broke down the front door.

Like an open tap, they had poured into the breach. Such was their desire to feed, that they even crawled over their own kind. He remembered hearing the cracking and snapping of bone as they surged up the stairs, like a waterfall in reverse.

Emma had become more forlorn then. He guessed that it was the maternal instinct kicking in to protect her young. No longer did she ask for help; she looked at him, gave him a resigned smile, then turned to face the onrushing tide of the festering dead. Like an

Olympic diver, she had cast herself from the top step, into the writhing mass of claws and jagged teeth.

At first, he thought she was fighting them off, but she just lay there, accepting her fate. Like vinegar sinking through olive oil, she disappeared into the grubby mass. While some stopped and rent her open, others kept on climbing the stairs.

Upwards.

Forever upwards.

It was only much later that he came to the conclusion she was trying to buy him time. Time enough to save their daughter, to keep her from the dreadful finality of this murderous host.

He saw Emma one last time, briefly exposed from within the frenzied mob devouring her whole. Blood had formed a shallow crimson pool in the hollow of her throat. Even as she was being pulled apart, she made no sound; there was only that same sad smile. Before her eyes rolled up, she mouthed one word, her final decree: "Go."

Snapping back to the world, he looked down into his daughter's eyes. Yet, as he tried to heave her up to the sanctuary of the attic, he could feel her slipping. Sweat ran down his arm, running under his fingers. He had grabbed her tighter, and she'd grumbled as he pinched her skin as he clung onto her forearm.

As Kerry was slowly brought up to the open hatch, he felt resistance. Looking beyond his daughter's face, now laced with trails of tears, he locked eyes on their next door neighbour. Lee. His daughter, a good few years older than Kerry, had babysat her on occasion. Lee's eyes were orbs of red and black. Teeth, with scraps of pink meat hanging from them, chomped the air beneath Kerry. One blood-soaked hand wrapped around her dainty leg.

Desperation kicked in as he tried to win this game of tug o' war. But for every inch he made, Lee repelled the advance. The landing was starting to fill up with the dead now. He had to do something, else his wife's death would've been in vain. He heard a yelp from Kerry, as his shoulder slammed into the wooden ridge around the hatch entrance. With both hands grabbing hold of his daughter, he managed to win the struggle and pull her up and away from the clamour below.

With his last ounce of energy, he rested her on a beam in the attic and rolled to one side. Sliding the hatch back into place, he lay there on his back. Laughter, a mix of hysteria and relief, rumbled from him, echoing around the musty loft.

As the wan light from the dim bulb flickered over them, he turned to Kerry. "Hey, don't worry, it'll be okay. It's just you and me now, kiddo. But we're safe up here, they can't get us." Still she cried, pushing the back of her hands into her eyes, rubbing them, feebly flailing at her face.

Sitting up, he held her hands before smoothing her hair down and pushing it behind her ears. "What's the matter, Boo? Are you sad about Mummy?"

Kerry shook her head.

"Is it Mister Teddy? Do you miss him? Don't worry, we can find another one."

Another shake of the head.

"Then what is it, Boo?"

Kerry lifted her leg up to show her daddy the bite mark on the back of her calf.

Ceepher shook away the image, realising that he was touching the grimy windscreen where the skeleton's eyes were looking back, trying to smudge the tears away. He wiped his hand on his jeans, pulled his cap down further, and turned back to the road.

All that remained now in this world was death.

CHAPTER FOUR

Ceepher jolted himself awake, just as the icy cold digits of the revenant, resident in his persistent nightmares, had slipped their way underneath and behind his eyes. He sat up, still groggy from the hold of slumber. The last beams of moonlight streaked in through the curtainless windows.

Within the ransacked house, he heard the timbers groan and creak, ghosts trapped within the fibre of the building, railing against the intruder in their home. Ceepher ignored the house's lament, knowing it was nothing more than the wind and neglect. Rummaging through his backpack, he placed the cardboard box package to one side, and delved deeper.

Where the hell is it?

His fingers wrapped around the thin metal flask, slowing down his heart. For a moment, he contemplated that he didn't need it at all, that it was just a form of muscle memory. Then the wraiths of the past wormed through his marrow, tugging at the knot within, trying to find a weak length of sinew it could tease free and seep back inside.

Necking a quick nip from the flask, the familiar warmth blazed a trail down to his near empty stomach. The paltry sustenance he had eaten the night before, after securing the building, long since subsumed into his muscle and bone. His cheeks flushed, and he took another, longer hit from the flask, before flopping back onto the sofa. Motes of dust floated around him; flakes of tissue paper skin from long dead people hovered in the beams of pristine moonlight.

One final slug, that was all he wanted. Enough to numb the mind, trick it into thinking that everything was of no importance, including his worth and his troubles. He slid the flask back inside the pack and slouched back into the fusty cushions.

The wall opposite had a framed picture, knocked to a jaunty angle. It showed a wonderfully captured vista of an English field in summertime. Yet for all its beauty, it was of no use to man in these days of simplicity. There would be time again for art and culture, but only when thoughts turned from merely clinging onto their fractured existence, and onto rebuilding.

Tilting his head sideways so that the painting appeared level, Ceepher felt himself being pulled into the fields of wheat. He could feel the sun on his face, hear birds chirruping in trees brimming with leaves and life. A tractor in the next field coughed, belching blackened wisps of smoke into the air. Opening his hands, he closed his eyes and walked amongst the tall stalks. Fingers raked across the bursting ears of wheat, seeds spilling from his touch and onto the ground.

A clang of metal and crash of glass made the calming scene disappear from view. His all too brief vacation retreated, dumping him back on the mouldy sofa in a dank house. He rolled his backpack over and pulled out the hatchet from the side panel. With a few intakes of breath, trying to invoke some life into tired lungs, he carefully stood up and edged towards the doorway.

There was another tinkling, as broken glass hit porcelain tiles, telling Ceepher that whatever it was, it was in the kitchen down the hall. He eyed up the front door to his right, still bolted and with the chain linked across to the frame. He reckoned that with a sharp tug, both would be pulled free from the rotten frame, but it would eat up valuable seconds.

For a moment, he contemplated getting his gear and heading upstairs, but the faint outline of a loft hatch at the top of the landing sent shivers down his spine.

The only sound was his shallow breathing, steady, rhythmic.

Sod it. If it was one of the deadheads, it could only be one, two tops. If it was anyone else, well…a grisly man looming at you with a raised axe in the middle of the night would tend to put the willies up most people.

Mind made up, he gripped the weapon tighter, counted to three, and then surged into the hallway. Within three steps he was by the kitchen doorway. Two more he was inside and by the rusting hob. He heard a gasp to his left, just beyond a tall cupboard which he had searched and found a decomposing pigeon within. Head bowed, he growled, turned and pointed the axe. "You made a mistake breaking in here tonight," he threatened. Two more steps and he was mere feet away from the dark alcove. As he went to swing, he saw a pair of glistening eyes in the gloom, stealing away his murderous intentions.

"Please," came a woman's thin reedy voice. "You have to help us."

The sentence stopped him completely. He gulped, "Us?" From the murk, the eyes manifested within a head, free from infection.

Still alive at least.

When he saw her near skeletal frame, it was clear that the woman had been living rough for some time. Her clothes were torn and flashed him bobbles of rib and sunken skin. She held one hand in front of her, as if she was trying to stop traffic. Her eyes bloomed and tears tracked down her gaunt face.

Ceepher relaxed, stood back and lowered the axe. "You said *us*. Where are the others?"

Gulping, the woman stuttered. "Just one more. Katie…show yourself."

From waist height, another pair of twinkling eyes appeared. A girl, no more than eight or nine, materialised, as if she was formed from shade. Her tangled greasy hair hung down over her shoulders. Unlike the woman, the girl's face wasn't sullen or afraid. She was smiling. "Hello, mister. Do you live here?"

He was taken off guard, and flitted between the woman and the girl, unsure if this was a cruel encore to his dream, or if it were real. "Wh…wh…what are you doing out here?"

The woman looked around frantically, searching the expanse of the room. "Please, you have to help us. They're after us, have been for days. I thought we'd lost them, but then th—"

She was interrupted by the sound of voices from outside. A flowerpot was smashed as clumsy feet knocked it over. It sent Ceepher's heart racing once more. The axe felt heavy, the cheap whisky which had staunched his memory now stymied his instincts. He looked from one set of eyes to the other; both were now milky billiard balls filled with fear.

Placing a finger to his lips, he beckoned them to him. "Stay close to me, let's go." Both of them nodded quickly. Clinging to each other, they slunk from the shadows and into the room. Out in the open, the woman's emaciated body was even more apparent. Ceepher wondered how they had survived for so long. How much longer would they be able to maintain their brittle hold on life?

He motioned them to crouch, and though the act seemed painful for the woman she did it without verbal complaint. The journey to the doorway was arduous. Each step seemed to make the house moan still further, as if it were trying to telegraph their location to the raiders outside.

When they got to the living room doorway, Ceepher pointed to the front door, and whispered, "Wait there." The woman shot out a hand, which latched onto his arm. Despite her slight build, her hold was firm. He looked her dead in the eyes. "I have to get my things, I'll be right back." The words seemed to comfort her a little, and he was able to peel her fingers from his jacket sleeve.

Inching into the room, he saw a beam of yellow light lance through the back window, in parallel to the moonlight from the front. He cursed under his breath and darted over to the sofa, making sure to pick up both the parcel and backpack.

Shoving the package inside his bag, he tiptoed back to the doorway. Clicking the rucksack clips together, he slung the bag over one shoulder. Voices surrounded the house; he could hear and feel the noose closing. He shimmied towards the front door. Trembling fingers fumbled for the chain, managing to free it from its catch. There was a loud crash from the kitchen as more glass was scattered over the tiled floor.

The voices outside grew louder, angrier, more desperate, calling out instructions and warnings. Ceepher waggled the bolt up and down, trying to release it from its clammy hold. As it popped out, the door did likewise, letting in cool air from outside. "When we get out, just run straight forwards. There's another house opposite us. There's an alleyway down the right hand side. Get there, we'll work our way out of the village one house at a time, okay?"

He received curt nods in reply. Pulling open the door, he went to let them past, only to discover that the exit was barred by a bearded man dressed in motorbike leathers. He leered at Ceepher, showing off the few teeth that home brew and cigarettes had yet to claim. "'Ello, me baba," he drawled.

The trio stepped back into the hallway. The man lurched towards them, crowbar in hand. Over the man's shoulder, Ceepher could see there was no one else lying in wait. Shoving the woman and child behind him, he swung the axe sideways, burying it in the man's chest.

The crowbar fell to the floor, quickly followed by its bearer, who held the head of the axe in his hands, trying to work out what the hell was going on. Ceepher placed a foot on the man's chest, heaved the axe out, and brought it down again. The head thwacked into the man's shoulder, near to his neck, and he let out a shrill cry, tried to plug the wound with filthy fingers. Ceepher kicked out at the assailant. A firm boot to the face pushed him onto his back. "Come on, let's go," he hissed at the woman and child. Cautiously, they edged their way out of the house and beyond the wounded man.

They reached the end of the gate, when behind them came a plaintive howling. Ceepher looked back to see the man trying to get to his feet. "Get to the house now! I'll be right behind you." As the pair headed towards the terraced houses opposite, Ceepher took a run up and kicked their assailant in the ribs. A jet of blood sprayed over the concrete, glistening in the early morning light. One hand tried to push himself up, but slipped on the slick fluid. His head hit the path and he fell still, beached in a growing puddle of his own blood.

CHAPTER FIVE

Ceepher guessed it was just after midday. The sun beamed down on them from above, drying out the sodden ground. Where the road was once his friend, he realised it could now lead to his downfall. They slunk through the undergrowth, cowering and ducking for cover at the slightest sound. The woman had introduced herself as Beatrice, though whether that was her real name or not, he couldn't decide.

She told him, in between ragged breaths from both exertion and angst, that she'd found Katie on a farm down in the Deverills. Of the girl's parents, she had asked of their fate only once, and received the silent treatment for two days. After that, seemingly convinced of her motives, the little girl had started to smile again.

This was around six months ago, though the exact length of time was a pure guess. Beatrice said that the ground had been frozen when she stumbled upon Katie hiding out in a barn. She was cowering within a skeletal cairn formed from the bones of livestock, beasts that had succumbed to starvation and pestilence. Since then, the pair had flitted across the countryside, surviving on water from rivers and what scant food they could scavenge.

Beatrice gave Ceepher a look when she said this, her eyes searching for that spark of recognition within the man, both knowing that there was nothing left in this wilderness. What little sustenance they found she had given to the girl, ignoring the grumbling of her own insides, the resistance from her atrophying muscle.

After dealing with a sole zombie, who fumbled for them, encased in vine and rope against the trunk of a tree, Ceepher checked the horizon and ushered his travelling companions to a small hollow by a crumbling stone wall.

He placed the package on the ground and checked his watch, saw that he still had a good chance of making his deadline before rooting within the bag. He pulled out a tin of corned beef and offered it to Beatrice. She studied it, as if it were an archaeological find of great importance. Fingers traced over the jolly farmer on the can's logo. A piece of straw stuck out of his mouth, bordered by mutton chop sideburns and a cheeky wink on his face.

Nodding thanks, she fumbled for the metal key and began to unfurl the lid. Ceepher allowed himself a hidden smile, for he hated corned beef. He'd only kept it as a last resort. It was good that it was going to someone who would appreciate it. "Hey, Katie, do you want s—" As he turned to check on the girl, he saw that she was shaking the parcel.

Snatching it from her, he whispered harshly, "Don't do that. It's not yours." The girl's face was crestfallen, her bottom lip began to wobble. Feeling a pinch of remorse, Ceepher, still clinging the parcel to his chest as if it were precious, eased up. "Hey, I'm sorry. I didn't mean to snap…just…I've got a job to do, and I don't want whatever is in here to get broken."

Wiping an invisible tear away, Katie huffed and picked at a clump of buttercups. Yanking the yellow petals off one by one, all the while looking at Ceepher, she sulked. "Hey, Katie, have some of this." Beatrice brokered a tentative ceasefire by shoving the open can of smashed up cow under the girl's nose.

Unable to both pout and deny herself food, she relented easily and grabbed the can. After shovelling in a mouthful, she looked across to Beatrice. "Thank you," she said proudly, before continuing to eat.

Ceepher mouthed his own thanks to the woman and began to repack his belongings. "So how long have you been out here?" Beatrice asked.

He stopped mid-flow. "A couple of years now. Not all the time. Just most of the time," Ceepher replied, before resuming his packing.

"How do you do it?"

He looked up at her. "Do what?"

"Stay around other people. After everything that happened? I mean…at any moment…they could just…you know…go funny again," she said, pulling her knees up to her chest.

"People only turn if the infected get you bad. Trick is to not let them. Most of the camps are pretty well defended now, least the ones I go to. Heard that big cities can be a different story altogether. It's best to avoid them if possible. Too many dead there…" He chuckled.

"What's so funny?"

Ceepher looked at the woman. "I still have to go there, though. You know. For jobs. Still, it's just me, so I can get in and get out quickly. As long as you don't go off adventuring, or try to dig up the past, you'll be okay."

As he placed the package back at the top of his bag, Beatrice pointed to it. "So what is it?"

He eyed her up, assessing any threat. He cast a quick glance at the girl, making sure she wasn't some kind of patsy. He pulled the top of the bag over and clipped it together. "No idea. I don't ask."

"Why not?"

"What difference does it make knowing?"

Beatrice pulled her knees in tighter. "I thought it would make all the difference knowing."

"Not to me. The minute you start filling your head with things other than getting from A to B, that's when…"

"What?" Beatrice asked, letting her legs fall to one side.

Ceepher looked from Katie, to Beatrice. "That's when things go wrong. My life is a lot easier when I just go from one place to another. I've got enough thoughts of my own, don't need the contents of any parcel…or other people adding to it."

Katie let out a burp, giggled and passed the half empty can to Beatrice. "I'm sorry for touching your stuff, Ceepher…why do people call you that?"

"Katie, don't be so rude," Beatrice snapped.

"Hey, it's okay. I don't mind. My little brother, well, I say little, he's only a year younger than me. When he was, I dunno, about your age, he couldn't say certain things properly."

"Like what?" Katie asked, spellbound.

"Like…squirrel, he would call it a squibble. I used to take the mickey out of him for that. Or dressing gown. He'd say dwessing gown, little stuff, you know. Used to make me laugh. My name is Christopher, except he couldn't say that either, so he'd call me Ceepher, and I guess it kinda stuck," Ceepher replied.

"That's funny," Katie agreed.

Ceepher nodded. "It used to make us laugh." For a moment there was silence; the sun fought to break through the tree canopy above them. The three of them looked at each other, and smiled. Beatrice licked her fingers clean and was just about to speak when they heard the sound of boots clumping on tarmac.

They each sunk to the floor, trying to ascertain the direction of the sound. All Ceepher could hear was his heart thumping inside his throat. "Stay here," he hissed. Crawling on his belly, he made his way to the wall, edging his way up its surface until he was level with a gap where a stone had fallen out.

He scoured either side of the road. Finally, to his right, the direction they had come from, he saw a leather-clad figure saunter down the road, idly swinging a length of chain. Cursing under his breath, he crept back to Beatrice and Katie. "There's at least one of them, we need to—"

Katie clamped a hand over her mouth and pointed behind Ceepher. Inching around, he followed where she was pointing, and saw a similarly dressed man walking in the field they were in, heading right for them.

Ceepher gripped his hair with his hands, tugging at it. He looked at the bag, and the road ahead. A signpost declared that Salisbury was a mere twelve miles away. For the briefest of moments he was consumed solely with the notion of flight. If he ditched them, he could easily outrun the hunters, leave the pair to their fate. He would be able to get to the delivery point with hours to spare.

Before he knew it, he had already pulled his backpack on, tightening the shoulder straps so it clung snugly to his body.

Just as he was about to spring from the ditch, abandoning the pair to the jackals, he saw Katie's face. It was ashen, mouth agape, trembling. In that moment he thought back to the attic, to when his own daughter revealed to him the bite mark.

He turned to Beatrice. "Hey, look, I'm going to try and distract them. I'll make a run for it, to the field over the road. When they go after me, go back where we came from, okay? Head towards Melksham. There's an old mobile home park there on the outskirts. Tell the guard that I sent you. He'll take you to meet a woman called Turner, tell her you know me, she'll keep you both safe."

"But what about you? We can't let you do—"

Ceepher held the woman by the shoulders. "There's no time. If they find you, there's no telling what they'll do. Trust me, just do what I say, okay?"

Reluctantly, she nodded and pulled Katie in closer. Ceepher sneaked to the wall again, and took a quick glimpse over the top. The biker was still sauntering down the road without a care in the world. He ducked down again, took in a deep breath before grabbing hold of the wall with both hands.

"Ceepher," Beatrice hissed. He looked across. "Thank you," she added.

Managing to fix his best reassuring smile to his face, he nodded, and vaulted over the wall. He landed cleanly, and sprinted across the road. As he broke cover, the chain-swinging biker yelled out, "Ee's over 'ere lads," and began to try to cut Ceepher off.

Beatrice looked up the field, and saw that the other man had also headed to the wall, and was easing himself over it. He joined in the shouting and disappeared from view. With a breath of relief, the pair began to work their way back where they had come from.

Ceepher made it to the wall bordering the empty field opposite to where they had been hidden. As he clambered over it, the crest cracked and gave way, sending him tumbling to the ground in a cloud of dust and rubble. A figure loomed over him, eclipsing the sun. He saw the chain flail in the air like a helicopter, before it smacked down on his head. Blackness enveloped him whole.

CHAPTER SIX

Ceepher took in a huge breath of air as a bucket of water was hurled over him. The tepid brackish stew was laden with twigs and dead bugs, which pelted against his skin. Taking in lungfuls of air, he shook his head.

"About time, fella. We tried a few friendly slaps, but you just didn't seem none too appreciative." Looking up, water dripping from his hair, Ceepher stared into the wide eyes of a man. His face was tanned, grooves carved into his skin from age and a lifetime of outdoor graft. A straggly beard bristled in time with the words.

"What do you want, grandad?" Ceepher asked, spitting out a mouthful of leaf mulch.

Fingers grabbed hold of Ceepher's hair. Twisting his head to one side, the bearded man leant in. "Not much for now. Just for you to be awake so we can begin your welcome tour." He pulled Ceepher's head back, throat taut. Every time he swallowed, it felt as if his Adam's apple was going to burst free.

Finally released, Ceepher took in his surroundings. He was in an old storeroom of some kind. A rusting roller door took up most of the wall opposite where he was seated. A length of chain swung gently, its links reflecting light from burning metal drums, which had been placed strategically around the interior.

Bent and buckled metal racking ran across the walls, makeshift weapons laid upon them, awaiting collection. Craning his neck around, he could make out a narrow doorway behind him, flanked by two guards, both dressed in motorcycle leathers. One wore an open faced helmet, a large spike protruding from the top.

A loud clang made Ceepher jolt to one side, to where the bearded man stood behind a hostess trolley. Keeping watch on his captive, the man hefted an array of tools, swinging them in the air, or rasping them against each other. The grinding metal set his teeth on edge, causing his captor to grin even more. Dropping a chisel on top of the trolley, he settled on a hand drill and made his way back to where Ceepher sat restrained in a metal chair.

"Poor old Norm, you fucked him up pretty bad. Doc reckons he might not be able to use his arm properly anymore. That wasn't very nice now, was it?"

Ceepher looked once more into the abyssal pits of the man's eyes, both of which seemed to pull what little light existed between the pair into them. "What was I supposed to do? Let him take me out? You look like you know what the fucking score is these days. It was him or me. You don't get anywhere if you think too much, especially out here."

The man pondered his words before shooting a grin, exposing black lined teeth. "I 'spose so. Still not gonna give Norm his wanking arm back, though, is it? I think it would be remiss of me not to make amends. An eye for an eye, an arm for an arm…" He held the drill in front of Ceepher's face, and wound the handle, spinning the drill bit up.

As the man loomed in closer, Ceepher could smell stale sweat and cheap booze. The sound of the whirring drill grew louder and louder. Stopping briefly, the effect complete, the bearded man placed the tip against the top of Ceepher's shoulder, before looking down at him. "Scream for me piggy."

At first, it was just a scratch, reminding Ceepher when he got his first tattoo. The sensation changed when he heard a popping sound, raising the intensity from one to ten in an instant. Unable to contain it, Ceepher howled. This just made the driller laugh. Flecks of spittle splattered Ceepher's face as his assailant began to turn the handle faster. Once it reached inside as far as possible, he pulled it free. A rope of blood and meat looped from the end of the bit to the wound, now a deep crimson.

This time, the man placed it into the freshly bored hole, horizontal to Ceepher's chest, so that the metal touched the inside of his shoulder blade. Winding slowly, he could feel every millimetre that the metal chewed into the bone. Flashes of agony shot up and down his body. He gritted his teeth so hard he feared they would shatter under the pressure.

As it built to a crescendo, Ceepher fell unconscious once more.

CHAPTER SEVEN

"Hey…wake up now."

His head felt heavy, as if he were drunk. Ceepher fought to lift it, but as he did, he looked into the madman's eyes once more. "There's a good boy. Now, if you're going to keep passing out, this is going to take a long time to get through. We've barely even started." He dug a finger into the wound in Ceepher's shoulder; the fingernail picked at the ravaged flesh within.

"What do you want?" Ceepher said, fighting back the pain.

Pulling his finger from the wound, the bearded man stuck it in his mouth and licked it clean. "We can't have people going around injuring our own, and not getting payback. You're going to be a warning to anyone else out there who thinks it's okay to not give us their shit. Like this, what the fuck is this?" In his free hand he held up a shiny metal drum, the same size as a small cask of beer. He rattled it in front of Ceepher's face; inside, there was a slight tinging against the metal canister.

"Where did you get that? That's not mine," Ceepher replied.

The man thumbed to a rack behind him, where a torn open box lay in tatters. "We found it in your little birthday present. Looks important. Not been able to get into it yet, but don't worry, we will. Unless you want to save us, and yourself, the trouble, and open it up?"

Ceepher coughed up a wad of blood and phlegm and spat it onto the floor by his side. "All I do is deliver the packages. I don't care what's in 'em." His forehead furrowed as he thought of something. "What time is it?"

Placing the metal object next to the ripped open cardboard box, the man walked across to a shuttered window and pulled on a metal chain, bathing the loading bay in light. Ceepher went to instinctively shield his eyes from the glow, but was held fast in the chair. The pull on his shoulder made him bite his lip.

The man strutted back. "Morning, I'd guess. Which means that we better get started again, wouldn't you say? We've had you for a few hours now, and your next of kin would still be able to recognise you." Lifting a lump hammer from the array of tools, the bearded man turned back to his prisoner. "Best change that, huh?"

As the hammer was raised, Ceepher clenched his eyes shut, bracing himself for the blow. From behind he heard a fevered argument, turn into yelling. The strike never came, and Ceepher dared to look. The bearded man had lowered his weapon and was looking over Ceepher's shoulder to the doorway. "What the hell is going on out there? Can't you see I'm busy?"

"Bulldog, it's…dead fucks…thousands of 'em," came the reply.

Looking down at Ceepher, Bulldog smirked. "Don't you be going anywhere now, Postman Pat. I'll be right back." He threw the hammer onto the tray, sending a number of tools flying onto the floor. Bulldog stormed past and out through the doorway.

A wave of nervous energy swamped Ceepher. He could feel his extremities tingle with adrenalin; his heart thudded in his chest. With the window shutter open, he looked around the room to see that it was indeed the loading bay to a shop of some kind. Browning posters hung from the walls, advertisements long since scoured from their surfaces by the sun and liberal application of fire and graffiti. With the guards departed, he was alone in the dusty room. Within the bowels of the building, he could hear heated arguments.

Flexing his wrists to test the bonds merely sent a flare of agony down his left arm. Still, he twisted his right wrist, and with the layer of sweat, felt that it had some give in it. Though it burned with every revolution, he continued to contort his hand, trying to free it.

Finally, having grabbed hold of the restraint with his left hand, he managed to slip free from the rope ties.

Carefully, not wishing to aggravate the gaping wound in his shoulder any further, he moved his hands to the front and massaged life back into them. After a few moments he undid the other wrist restraint before tackling the knots around his ankles and standing up gingerly. The first few steps reminded him of a wildlife programme he'd seen before the Day of the Zed, where a newborn calf, still covered in gunk, stumbled around its stall.

Shuffling over to the selection of torture implements, he rooted through them, settling on a serrated steak knife. Though it was rusting, the teeth were sharp, as his thumb could testify to. As he tucked a claw hammer into his belt, and a screwdriver into a pocket, he heard something strike against the revealed window.

With the beams of morning light streaking through the grimy window, Ceepher shielded his eyes and walked towards it, taking care to not trip over the myriad obstacles. When he was a few feet away, he heard the sound again. A green hand, with crimson fingers, pawed at the glass.

Instinctively, he stepped backwards, raising the knife, ready for an attack which never came.

The hand was joined by another, and another, until it looked like he had a cadre of adoring fans outside the building, eager to meet him and press the flesh. Amongst the decaying limbs he saw heads in varying stages of rot and damage. One, with the entire side of its skull caved in, looked back dumbly with its one remaining eye. As it clocked the fresh meat inside, its jaw clacked open and shut like a castanet.

As the cacophony grew, the roller door shutters began to boom to a discordant beat. Standing in the middle of the room, the banging surrounded him, bearing down incessantly. From behind, a familiar voice shouted, "How the fuck did you get free?"

Ceepher spun round, weapon raised, to see Bulldog entering the room. Before he could answer, two more lackeys walked in, dragging a writhing body between them. Dumping him on a workbench, one of the men left, a hand clamped over his mouth, struggling to hold his screams hostage inside his lungs, leaving the other to take care of the stricken man.

Bulldog and Ceepher stared each other down, before the remaining guard coughed to interrupt. "Boss, what are we gonna do with Georgie? He don't look too good." Tearing his gaze away, Bulldog stormed over to the workbench and shoved the guard out of the way.

Daring to see what was up with the wounded man, Ceepher edged closer, trying to get a peek. Standing on a raised section of concrete, he managed to look across and saw that the man was in a bad way. His jacket had been torn open. The zip hung like a chain from a pocket watch. A previously white vest had been ripped to shreds, along with the man's torso. In amongst the gouges were white flashes of rib, pulsing organs and stringy black sinew.

The man's face was pale, save for a bloodied hand print pressed neatly against his skin, as if it were done intentionally. He was panting, mumbling incoherent sentences, his face twitching with ticks and flinches.

Bulldog lifted up the bloodied rags from the man's chest before pressing his fingers to the wound. Rubbing them together, he gave them a sniff before recoiling. He looked across to the guard, who stood there wringing his baseball cap. "He's spoiled meat now, Pete. Infected. There's only one thing we can do with Georgie now, isn't there?"

Pete nodded disconsolately, looking to the floor. Bulldog placed a conciliatory hand on the guard's shoulder, whilst simultaneously pulling free a bayonet from a sheath on his belt. After a playful slap to Pete's face, he nodded, stood over George's twitching body, and placed the bayonet against the temple.

It was then that George opened his eyes. Ceepher had unknowingly trudged over to the gathering, reeled in by the macabre show. He could see that Bulldog was right; the tell-tale signs of infection had already made the blood vessels in the man's eyes look like red spider webs, tributaries of crimson ichor.

George looked up to Bulldog, licked his cracked lips, before asking weakly, "Mum?"

Bulldog shook his head softly. "No, son, it's not your mum. It's the reaper, he's come for you." George looked back blankly. His hands began to curl inwards, into tensed balled claws. As they began to raise up, Bulldog placed one hand on the top of George's forehead, pinning him to the workbench, before pushing the bayonet into the skull.

There was a wet gasping sound as George sucked air down his throat, into rent open lungs. Fingernails scratched against the metal bench, trying to resist the pull of the void beyond. Bulldog pushed the blade in until it rested against the hilt. With his palm on the end, he twirled the bayonet around like a blender. For a moment the keening of bone against metal reached a new high pitch, before it ended with a pent up sigh from George.

Hands fell slack and slipped off the bench, swinging briefly before coming to a rest. Bulldog looked across to Ceepher. "We're completely surrounded. They're twelve deep out front, at least. Not too sure how long the barricades are going to last before those fuckers get in."

Ceepher shrugged. "And? You were halfway to crippling me a minute ago, what do you want now?"

Bulldog rested George's hands on his bloodied chest, closed the man's wide open eyes before resting a hand on the head once more. "If we are to have any chance of seeing this through, we'll need everyone, including bastards like you." Gripping the bayonet's handle, he wrenched it free. It exited with a slurp, and a slurry of brain and bone spilled onto the floor.

"It doesn't look like I have much of a choice, huh?" Ceepher asked.

Shaking his head, Bulldog cleaned the blade on George's trousers before slipping the weapon back in its sheath. "Nope, not much. The way I see it, I can kill you now or you can wait and the deaders will do it for you."

"Wow, that's a tempting offer. You're a real big time negotiator, huh?"

Bulldog shrugged.

"I'd rather die on my feet than on my knees, though your little DIY has restricted me somewhat." Ceepher leant forward, showing the gaping hole in his shoulder.

"I'll send you up to the doc. He can patch you up. I'll let the others know that you're with us. Norm won't be too happy, but the way he's looking, not sure how long he's going to last anyway," Bulldog said.

Nodding to the guard, the pair went to leave. Ceepher stopped Bulldog on the way out, "If we get through this, we're square, yeah?"

Bulldog grinned. "Pal, once you see what we're up against, you'll see that *if* is a mighty fucking long way away."

CHAPTER EIGHT

"Have you ever seen that many before?" the Doc asked.

Ceepher grimaced as a liberal slug of antiseptic was sloshed over the shoulder wound. "No…only from the videos on the internet, before the power went." The pair looked out from the second floor window, to a sea of groping hands and pallid sallow skin. Even from the height, they could tell which ones had been infected on day one, and which were the victims of that initial wave of cannibalism.

News reports had speculated over the exact method of delivery of the virus, by the pro-planet group, 'One World, No People'. Some blamed it on an aerosol, which was sprayed over a number of urban areas, whilst others purported it to be a waterborne agent, introduced into the reservoirs. Regardless of the method, the effect was devastating. Within two days of the identification of 'Patient Zero', it was already too late.

Those early days of scattered reports of family members killing and eating their children and partners became commonplace. Soon, you weren't seeing the infected on television; they were in your street, banging at your front door in full glorious 3D.

There seemed to be a difference between the infected and those that were reanimated after being attacked by them. Whilst the infected, those who had ingested the bioweapon, were more aggressive, less inclined to skip a meal, the people who managed to escape them, albeit wounded, became part of a horde. They were more like cattle, moving from one location to the next, following the plaintive moans of their kind to find the next meal.

Within a matter of weeks, these lumbering cadavers outnumbered the infected. All they needed was to break the skin, get one morsel of their infected tissue into you, and that was it, game over. A short gestation period of excruciating pain and agony changed anyone into one of the deaders. There was only one way to kill them. Remove the head or destroy the brain.

Ceepher had found this out in the crawlspace above his house, whilst cowering from the shambling undead, the pair reduced to being squatters in their own home. Kerry had developed a bad fever, and nothing he could do would placate her. He had resorted to using balled up socks as a gag to try to keep her screams from riling them up.

Exhaustion had robbed him of consciousness, and when he came to, his daughter was quiet, bundled up under a musty blanket against one of the walls. Her face was covered, and for the briefest of moments he dared to hope that she was somehow okay, that she was immune, or that it was just a terrible nightmare.

Then the blanket unfurled, and she was revealed. Though it looked like his little Boo, the veins criss-crossing her body were lines of tar, scored into pale blue skin. Hands, ending in little claws, reached for him, fetid breath prefaced a low moan as her eight-ball eyes looked at him dispassionately. He was catatonic. This couldn't be happening, not to Kerry, not his little girl. Patting himself for something he could use as a weapon to defend himself, he realised that, despite the other supplies, he didn't have one thing he could use.

Resigned, he sat against the far wall, waiting for the end. Kerry took one lumbering step forward, off the beam she was resting on, and onto the plasterboard floor. A surprised yelp escaped from her maw as she disappeared through the ceiling and into the bathroom below, followed by a loud cracking sound.

Wiping his tears away, Ceepher crawled across the wooden struts to where Kerry had been seconds earlier. A perfectly rectangular hole formed between the wooden roof beams.

And there she was.

Her descent had been halted by the bathtub, her neck bent back to an impossible angle. Her tiny body sprawled lifelessly in the enamel tub, whilst her dead eyes looked back up at him. Spindles of bone protruded from her pale neck, like an ornate necklace. Congealing lumpy black sludge oozed from where the bones stuck out, sliding down into the bath. A few of the undead were in the room already, drawn by the commotion. Their moans sounded disappointed, as if they felt they had been robbed of something to feed on.

He couldn't tear himself away from the view.

Her face was no longer full of malice, replaced instead by an ambivalent smile. He wondered if it was relief of her corporeal escape, or some cosmic joke that he wasn't a part of. It was only when one of the zombies below tried to swipe his face off that he pulled away.

It was that smile which haunted him over the next three months, prying at his sanity. Only alcohol could cover it. He sought solace in the flat above his old local, 'The Red Lion'. He near drank the place dry before he was found and offered his first job. He was given a purpose at last, a reason to carry on. It filled up his days, and whilst others discounted his job due to the occupational hazards present, the threat of death never bothered him.

He had nothing left which could be taken.

The doc stuck the needle through a ragged piece of skin, Ceepher hissed in pain. "You in the land of the living? Began to wonder where you went," the doctor said wryly.

Ceepher looked out across the horde; like coral in a reef being moved by the tide. "I'm here alright. Your bedside manner is making sure of that."

Smiling, the doc continued to weave needle and thread through the patches of skin, hitching them together. "Not long now and you'll be good to go. I wouldn't partake in any arm wrestling matches, but the stitches should hold for a while. Here." In his open hand, the doc held a plastic bottle which rattled like a child's toy.

Ceepher opened it up and saw two red and white capsules at the bottom. "For the pain," the doc said. With a final flourish, he tied a knot in the end, snipped the suture thread off, and began to pack his equipment away.

Nodding a thanks, Ceepher began to dress himself. "What was this place? You know, before the fall? Looks like a shop or something."

The doc closed his bag up and clicked the clasps into place. "Three little shops in the middle of an old council estate. There's a launderette one side, a bookies the other. This was one of those household recycling places. It's called 'Rorke's Thrift'." He smiled as he spoke.

Ceepher chuckled. Looking out at the burgeoning throng of zombies below, he said, "How wonderfully apt."

"If you two have finished, there's work to do. The security gate isn't going to hold much longer. We need to start thinning the ranks," Bulldog's unmistakeable voice said from behind them.

Standing up and straightening out his clothes, Ceepher flexed his arm. The pain was numbed, for now at least. "Fine, tell me what you need doing."

CHAPTER NINE

Ceepher was led down the stairs, through a winding corridor, past a dilapidated small kitchen, to the shop itself. The shelves were bare. Any goods that weren't looted in the first few days were lying in pieces against one of the far walls. The entire length of the shop—which served as the main front display—was missing its one key constituent component: glass. If it weren't for the safety gate—a flexible wall made of metal with gaps the size of house bricks—being down, the humans inside would have likely been eaten or infected already.

The moaning was deafening. Hands flailed at the sight of the five bikers already in the shop, staying out of reach, and lashing out at anything that came near. As Bulldog and Ceepher entered, they stood upright, as if their supervisor had come in to check on them. Given the sheer weight of numbers of the undead in the car park out front, the gate flexed inwards, the links audibly straining under the pressure.

Bulldog passed Ceepher a metal gate pole, one end sharpened to a wicked point, and a bundle of cable ties. The second item made the courier frown. "Okay, ladies and germs, listen up. These dead fucks are going to get in here, unless we start to thin them out. As you can see, whilst this safety gate is keeping them out, their murderous little bastard hands can get in. We don't want to be at home to Mister Fuck-Up now, do we?"

A chorus of mumbling and huffing signalled everyone was in agreement.

"Good, I suggest we cable tie their hands together so that they can't grab us, or even worse, scratch us. If you've got gloves, wear them, if not…well, put it this way…if I so much as suspect that you've been infected, I'll bash your head in as soon as look at ya.

"If we work in batches, we should be able to restrain those at the front, which should then stop those at the back sticking their grubby little mitts in. Then I suggest you start to kill them as quickly as you can. Any questions?"

A man wearing a bandana and sunglasses raised his hand. "What about the back, boss? What do we do about them?"

Bulldog pulled out a pair of leather biker gloves and started to put them on. "For now, there isn't much we can do. They're pressed up against the roller doors, but they seem to be holding. These bastards are our priority. Let's try to deal with them first, then we'll see what we can do about the others. Anyone else?"

The others checked over their weapons. A few dared to look at the wall of hands and arms reaching for them through the gate. "Good, now, let's get to it," Bulldog said.

Ceepher searched his pockets, found his own gloves and pulled them on, before pushing down on each finger, making sure they were on tight. The others were advancing cautiously towards the keen shoppers outside. Bulldog was a different story. He marched towards the closest zombie, a man dressed in a tracksuit that was disintegrating from the decomposing corpse's body.

Without a care in the world, he grabbed both hands and looped a semi-closed cable tie around them, pulling it together before the walking maggot farm could do anything other than chew thin air. The zombie bit the air in annoyance. Bulldog brought the metal pole down and snapped the tied arms downwards, breaking them and leaving them flopping uselessly around. His gloved hand reached through the gate, grabbed hold of the zombie by the throat, and pulled it flush up to the metal links.

Resting the pole between his legs, Bulldog slipped a finger behind one of the zombie's eyes. A quick flick scooped the orb free from the socket. He repeated the trick on the other side before threading a cable tie through each socket. Pulling each end, the skull was held against the gate. He zipped the ties together and pulled tightly, forming a firm hold. With its eyes dangling from their respective sockets, and its hands lashed together, the zombie let out a moan, yet still railed against its treatment.

Ceepher worked methodically from the far right hand side. Before he tackled each pair of hands, he looped the cable tie together, so all he had to do was slap the hands together, slip it over them and pull taut. The first few worked fine, but the fourth must've been out there for a while. As he closed the hands together, ready to get the cable tie in place, the zombie pulled back. As it did, and with Ceepher gripping the hands tightly, the skin covering each hand came off like a pair of latex gloves.

Swallowing back vomit, Ceepher threw the skin mittens to the floor, shoved the cable tie over the skeletal hands down to the wrists, and pulled tight. The plastic bit through the sallow flesh and decaying meat and tendons with ease, stopping only when they pressed the bones together.

Bulldog laughed. "You got a juicy one there, pal." He dodged a desperate lunge from one of the zombies, and retaliated with a punch, which broke the creature's nose. "That was a close one t—"

He was interrupted by a scream. They all looked over to Ted, who was working over on the far left. His weapon clattered to the ground as he squeezed the palm of a hand with his fingers. Bulldog finished up with his current victim, before pushing his way across to the yelping man.

The closer he got, the more Ted realised what was about to happen. He began to plead, "No, boss, it's fine, it's nothing, I must've caught it on a jagged piece of metal. I'm fine. Honest."

Stopping by him, Bulldog loomed over Ted like a shark in an aquarium. "Let me see, Teddy boy."

Cautiously, Ted held his hand out, revealing a two-inch gash from below the middle finger all the way to his wrist. Already the blood was bubbling and thickening. Bulldog held the hand, examined it, before holding it up and turning it around in the light. "You're right, it's just a nick, you're going to be fine."

Ted sighed, and inclined his head. "Thanks, boss. I knew it—" His sentence was punctuated by a metal pole lancing through the bottom of his jaw, up through his entire skull. It protruded from the top of his head like an old German WW1 Pickelhaube helmet. For a few moments, he mimed silent words. As he wordlessly opened his mouth, the others could see the bloodied metal pole running through the back of his throat.

Bulldog yanked the spike free and let Ted collapse to the ground before turning back to the men. "Get back to it you lot. We've got a job to do. Don't fuck up like Teddy boy here, okay?"

Nodding, they resumed their task, and finished up restraining the groping hands.

CHAPTER TEN

With no further mishaps, they were able to subdue the zombies sticking their hands through the safety gate. A few of the undead—torn in half and trying to grab the men by the ankles—were also dealt with. Bulldog looked up and down the line approvingly. "Good work you lot. Now, the fun bit. Let's go crack some skulls."

With a degree of zeal and relish, the men shoved the unused cable ties in their pockets and retrieved their weapons. Methodically, they moved the tied hands to one side, and rammed the spiked poles into the zombies' heads. Most aimed for the eyes, trying to lance them through the soft orbs and directly into the brain, save trying to break the skull itself.

Ceepher started to work his side. As each of them was dealt with, it was as if a candle inside them had been extinguished. They sunk towards the floor, their journey halted by their bound hands.

With the front line dealt with, their place was taken by the one behind, and so the cycle continued. Within ten minutes, there was a wall of dead bodies forming in front of the safety gate. The undead, in their eagerness to get at the fresh meat in front of them, stepped over their fallen kin. When they too were despatched, they were added as aggregate to the foul barricade being made by their corpses.

Still they came.

Relentless.

Desperate.

No instinct other than to clamber over the bodies in front of them in a vain attempt to try to snag one of the breathers inside. Bulldog shouted out, "Take five minutes lads. Get something to drink. I'm gonna take a look upstairs and see what we're left with." He pointed to Ceepher. "Come on, pretty boy. Let's have a butchers."

From the upstairs window, the pair looked down onto the car park. "Fuck a duck, there's still hundreds of them. Where are they all coming from?" Bulldog asked.

Ceepher peeked over the window sill at the devastation they had wrought. Already there was a fresh batch of zombies trying to push their fetid limbs through the wall of dead bodies arranged in front of them. "It's like they're being drawn here."

"But by what? Or whom?" Bulldog asked, looking at Ceepher suspiciously.

"Hey don't look at me, pal. I've never had this problem before. I'm not trying out some weird new aftershave," Ceepher replied, holding his hands out.

Bulldog grumbled under his breath, before he added, "Regardless, there's something in here that is pulling them in. We need to find out what it is, otherwise they *will* get in, and I've got better things to do today than get ripped to shreds by a bunch of dead fucks."

"Like what? Rape? Pillage? Murder?"

"Those are a few of my favourite things," Bulldog said. He shot Ceepher a maniacal grin, before stomping off downstairs.

For a moment, Ceepher stood there and simply watched as the undead crawled and writhed their way over the slaughtered herd. He looked down the main road and saw that even more were shuffling their way towards them. He hated to admit it, but Bulldog was right; something was drawing them here.

Then it hit him. He looked at his watch and saw that it was ten in the morning. Not only was he late for his delivery, something he'd never been before, but he realised when it had all started.

Forty eight hours, no more. That bastard Kipworth had sent him on a suicide mission. Whatever was in that package had to be what was causing this. He spun on his heels and darted down the stairs, out to the loading bay. The moaning was louder in there too. The roller doors appeared to be buckling under the pressure.

He scanned the racking and saw the shiny metal object. It didn't weigh much. He rapped on its side with his knuckles; it sounded hollow. Turning it over, he saw that there was no obvious way in, no screws, no joins or seam, nothing. Looking across to a window, he had a thought.

Ceepher placed the canister against the middle of the window. On the other side, hands continued to slap at the safety glass, trying to get in. He then rolled it to one side, the hands followed. Whatever was in there, only the dead were aware of it. Sitting down in the chair he had not too long ago been tied to, Ceepher turned it round in his hands, locating a faint set of markings on the bottom. Trying to get a glimmer of light on it, he made out three words: 'His Majesty's Government'.

CHAPTER ELEVEN

Ceepher set the canister down on the rack. He had to find a way out of here, clear a path to safety. All he needed was some kind of distraction. If he could get past the zombies, then he could make a break for it, hope that whatever was in the canister was a stronger pull than he was.

"Come on dickweed, we've got a job to do, " Bulldog yelled from the doorway.

Standing up, Ceepher started to follow before a thought hit him. "I'm just going to check on Norm. We don't want any surprises coming for us when we're working downstairs."

Bulldog waved a hand. "Knock yourself out, pal. Just hurry up. They're getting thicker again at the front."

Taking the stairs two at a time, Ceepher rounded the corner and headed towards a small room on the first floor. Inside, on a row of palettes, lay the man he had axed earlier. Ceepher closed the door carefully behind him and tiptoed over to the wounded man. Yellow and red bandages ran around his torso; sweat mingled in with the blood making it look like a liquid Battenberg mix had swaddled him.

For a moment, Ceepher was worried it was too late, that the man had already died and was beginning to turn into one of the walking dead. Then Norm opened his eyes. "It's you…come back…to finish what you started huh? Go ahead mate…be…my guest…"

Ceepher walked over to a pair of large double glazed windows and, after a bit of elbow grease, managed to push them open. He looked down to see the rear roller doors; a mosh pit of hungry zombies waited beneath him.

"Come on, *mate*, let's go make something useful out of you," Ceepher whispered in Norm's ear. He dug his hands under the injured man's armpits and hauled him off the palettes and towards the window.

The stitches in his shoulder began to pull and strain. He looked down and saw a patch of red bloom on his t-shirt. Norm tried to struggle, but between his wounds and the fever, put up little fight. Ceepher lifted Norm up and rested his stomach against the windowsill, so that the top of his body flopped out of the open window.

With a cool breeze blowing on his face, Norm took in a deep lungful of fresh air before realising his predicament. "What are you doing?"

Ceepher took a moment to collect himself, then he began to ease the wounded man out of the window, holding an ankle in each hand. Norm was now upside down, mere feet from the braying mob of zombies, who could sense that, although this one wasn't as fresh as could be, he still had some good eats on him. All they had to do was pry him open.

Ignoring both Norm begging for his life, and the searing agony in his shoulder, Ceepher began to swing the man by his ankles. With enough momentum built up, and aiming for a large dumpster to one side of the roller doors, he launched Norm through the air and watched as he landed on top of the large bin.

In a daze, Norm tried to pick himself up, but one leg was dangling over the side. A keen member of the undead group seized hold of the warm flesh and burrowed its fingers through the skin and into the tender meat. Norm went to scream, but another zombie stuck bony talons into his throat and pulled the meaty pipe out. As he gurgled on his own fluids, he patted the side of the dumpster.

Ceepher could see that the shoal of monsters were ambling towards the offering. With a gap created, albeit a small one, he knew that it was now or never. He dangled out of the window, allowing his good arm take the weight. Not wanting to hang around, he let go and landed heavily.

The air was pushed from his lungs, but something inside commanded him to get up, to go. He rolled under a clumsy swipe from a dead woman dressed in a bear outfit, who was clutching a sign advertising two for one cocktails, and picked himself up. He saw that the rear gate, a big heavy industrial thing, was wedged shut. Vaulting up the wall, he sat on top and looked back at Norm.

The man had already been pulled apart; the lucky few who had gotten there early were feasting on a whole arm, swatting away would-be interlopers, intent on stealing a finger or two. Ceepher swivelled and looked beneath him. There was no one there, just thick grass leading to a forest. Rules be damned, he'd have to chance it, hope he could pick a path to a safe zone.

As he was about to jump off, he heard a voice shout from the building behind him. "OI! Where do you think you're going? Get back here, you piece of shit."

Ceepher smiled, turned around slightly and gave him the finger. "Hey, numbuts, go fu—"

From within the loading bay, a timer struck zero inside the canister; an electrical pulse flashed through a series of wires before sparking life into a detonator. The explosion ripped through the building, vapourising all within. The back-blast flattened the horde outside, knocked Ceepher from his perch and into the undergrowth.

CHAPTER TWELVE

---CLASSIFIED REPORT---
---Test X10 Complete---
---Location 51.1930° N, 1.9027° W---
---Efficiency 93.47%---
---MESSAGE ENDS---

Kipworth eyed the courier up. "Don't see many women doing deliveries these days. Here, take a few extra bands. Looks like you and your daughter need something to eat." After shoving some elastic bands in her hand, he waved her away, as if she were an irritating wasp.

He studied the brief report again, before pulling a map from a briefcase. Smoothing it out, he read the co-ordinates once more. "Hmmm, Shrewton eh? Not quite what we were after, but an adequate test nonetheless. I guess you get what you pay for these days."

Replacing the report and map back in his case, he sighed contentedly. It had been a good day. He glimpsed into his pint glass once more. What was that?

Another piece of rodent perhaps?

Maybe even a scrap of rubber or a piece of junk?

No matter, it was one of life's little pleasures, sampling the local wares. He drank as much as he dared, without revealing the mysterious object, deciding that some things are better left unknown. "What you don't know, can't hurt you," he said aloud, allowing himself a wry smile.

Placing the glass down on the bar, he waved thanks to the bartender. With one hand resting on the bar, he went to stand up just as a rusting steak knife was slammed down through the back of his hand, pinning him to the wood.

Try as he might, he couldn't pull it free. He turned around to see his attacker. "Hello, Kipworth. I told you what would happen if you jerked me around, didn't I?"

Ceepher waved at Beatrice, who led Katie outside. "But she's…" Kipworth mumbled.

The rest of the clientele went back to their business. Holding up a bucket full of scrumpy, Ceepher waved it under Kipworth's nose. "It was the only thing I could find that was big enough for this particular rat's head." He butted the back of Kipworth's head with the axe handle, knocking him against the bar top.

As the barman's hand squeaked inside another glass, Ceepher raised the axe and swung downwards.

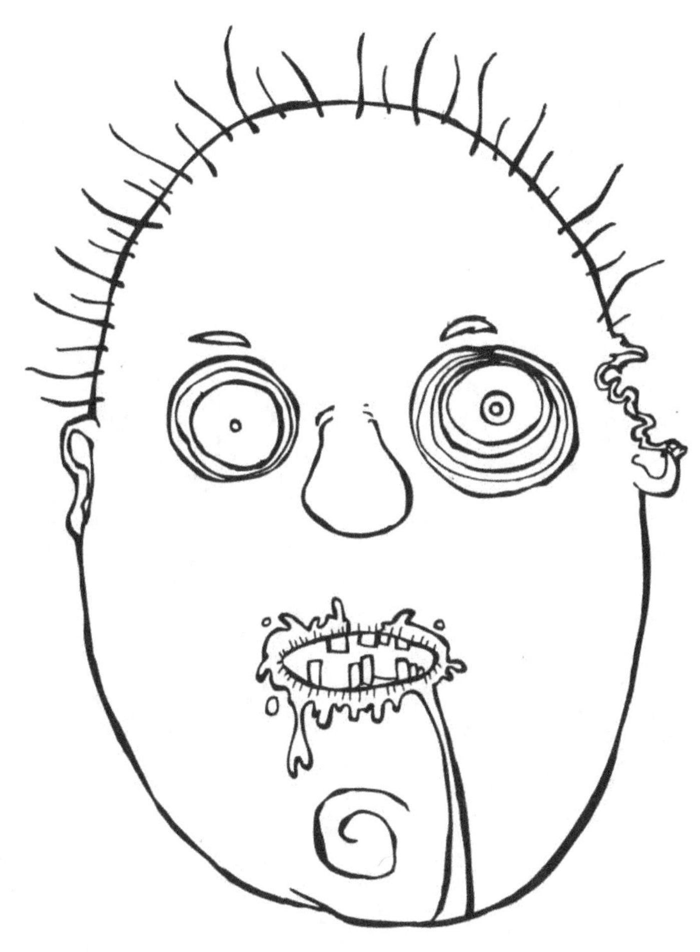

CHARITY BEGINS AT HOME

With the doorbell still echoing through the hallway, beyond the scratched and pitted wooden front door, Sadie looked at her clipboard before turning back to the street. It looked like so many of the terraced rows of houses, estates and cul-de-sacs she spent her days traipsing up and down. Both ends were still barricaded with burnt-out cars, wheelie bins and anything else bulky enough to lash together to form some kind of semi-permanent fortification.

The remaining cars on the street were effectively landlocked, but given that fuel was rationed, along with seemingly everything else, no one was kicking up a fuss right now. With the evening closing in, the lampposts began to flicker and pop into life, humming like a swarm of incarcerated insects. Every other one remained off; all part of the national push to conserve energy.

Plumes of smoke from still-smouldering tower blocks made the air taste bitter, and hung over the city like a shroud. It had been hard enough to see the stars twinkle overhead *before* the world had been devoured, but the smog now completely obscured the sky. Even the moon struggled to shine a path through.

Sadie turned back to the house and knocked on the door, daring to peek through the living room window. The net curtains twitched, revealing a woman in her fifties looking back nervously. With rollers in her hair, and a cigarette precariously balanced in her mouth—in danger of lighting up the hanging soft furnishings—she shook her head once, before pulling the curtains to. Shutting out the world for another day.

"Understandable," Sadie murmured to herself. She drew a line through number eighty eight, and headed back down the path. Rumour was that most of the residents of Brown Street had remained. Right from Day One, to the conclusion some seven months later. They'd gotten used to hiding behind closed curtains and bolted doors, under siege by their former neighbours and friends.

One house remained in the street. Sadie opened the gate to number ninety, and left it open. A number of occasions now, she had been forced to make a hasty retreat after an errant dog escaped from a house and chased after her. The front door was UPVC and, compared to the rest of the street, was near immaculate. She was indentured to the sight of bloodied handprints, or clumps of dried meat and hair splattered over the surface.

After a quick check, she found no doorbell. She grabbed hold of the knocker and rapped it four times. From within, she could hear the radio blaring, set to the ubiquitous City Zen station. It provided half hour news updates, and, up until recently, regular incident reports on gatherings of the infected.

Four frosted glass panels set into the top of the door had a warm beige glow. A shadow moved across it, and Sadie heard the metal covering the spyhole slide across the plastic inside.

Following myriad bolts being removed, and chains sliding free, the main lock cracked, and the door opened a sliver to reveal a man's face. He was wearing thin metal-rimmed glasses, and what little hair he had remaining was slathered across his head in a sparsely thatched comb over. "Yes?" a reedy voice asked.

Sadie wished she had a tape recorder for this bit, the script known off by heart. "Good evening, sir. My name is Sadie, and I'm collecting on behalf of HOARD, I—"

"Who?" he asked tersely.

She sighed. one in two people who actually bothered to open the door asked her this question. "HOARD. Helping Orphans Affected by the Reanimation Disease. We're government approved, and I'm here tod—"

"HOARD?"

"Yes, sir. H-O-A-R-D."

"Well surely if you're from the Helping Orphans Affected by the Reanimation Disease people, you should be called H-O-A-B-T-R-D?"

Oh great, one of these.

"I think the B and the T are silent, so as to make an acronym which is easy to remember, sir."

"What? HOARD?"

"Yes, sir."

"So, let me get this right, young lady. The government thinks that, after surviving everything we have in this country, some brainiac decided it was a good idea to create a charity that sounds phonetically the same as *horde*? You know, a mass of infected people, hellbent on eating you?" he replied, opening the door a little further.

Sadie clutched her clipboard to her chest, raised it defensively. "I'm sorry to have disturbed you, sir. Have a good evening." Spinning on her heels, she drew a line through number ninety, knowing that she could at least get home in time for her unarmed combat training session.

The door whooshed open; Sadie retreat into herself, fearing some form of physical reprisal. The man, now completely revealed, was about as threatening as a puddle. He was wearing trousers, shirt, and a striped tie, held back behind a light grey cardigan. "I'm sorry, I didn't mean to offend. It's just…you know…we don't get many people round any more. Ha, months back it was looters, then it was…*them*, the last thing I expected was some do-gooder."

Sadie relaxed slightly, allowing her arms to fall to her side. "It's fine, I understand, I do, I'm just trying to do my bit. You know?"

Smoothing down his cardigan, he swung his fist playfully in the air. "You betcha, young lady." Realising that the last time any of his attempts at social interaction were considered 'okay' was thirty years ago, he blushed and looked to the ground, castigating himself under his breath.

"Hey, it's okay. I appreciate it. Thank you," Sadie chirped.

The man pushed his glasses up the bridge of his nose and smiled, revealing a gap between his top two front teeth. "Phew, I didn't mean to offend you. So…now that that misunderstanding is out of the way, what can I do for you? We don't have any money I'm afraid…not that money is worth anything these days, I suppose…" The man trailed off into nothingness.

Sadie put her best smile back on and walked back down the path. Standing directly in front of the man, she realised she was a good couple of inches taller than him. "Of course. Well…I'm collecting for the orphans. If you have any spare, we'd love some ration slips, maybe for things that you don't need? We had some kids' clothes ration slips delivered to us at home. Must've been old records, I guess, you know…before everything? So, we gave them to HOARD."

The man scratched his nose, then withdrew his finger, perhaps worried that she would misconstrue the act as a casual spot of nasal mining. "Oh…of course. You know, I'm not sure, but I think we might have something. Why don't you come in a minute and I can take a look?"

Sadie sucked in air. "We don't really go into people's houses, just in case they are—"

"Nutjobs?" the man replied enthusiastically, before again realising that his tone was a little peculiar. "Sorry," he added.

Another awkward silence fell, broken by the sound of a muted beeping from inside the house. The man's face dropped. "Oh poppycock! My dinner!" He spun around and waddled back into the house at speed, leaving Sadie stranded on the doorstep.

Cautiously, she tiptoed towards the open front door, daring a peek inside. She saw that the wooden floor had been polished to within a millimetre of its existence. A long thin rug ran the length of the hallway, like a beige runway. She was gobsmacked. The place was immaculate.

Wallpaper was hung expertly, with no visible joins. A table sat against a wall in the middle of the hallway; a telephone, pad and pen rested on top of a delicate lace doily, set out as if it were a show home. A thick cream carpet ran upstairs, covered with plastic sheeting. From within the house, the beeping stopped.

After a few seconds, the man appeared from the kitchen at the back of his house. Even from distance, Sadie could see that his forehead was sheened with a thin veil of sweat. "Phew, got there in time. No harm, no foul," he said breathlessly.

Standing level with the stairs and a doorway, he straightened himself out and checked his appearance in a mirror, dabbing a hankie over his head to absorb the perspiration.

"Come on, dear, don't be shy. You're already in now," he said, pointing to Sadie. She looked down to see that she had absentmindedly walked into the house, drawn to its spotlessness.

"Oh…sorry, I didn't mean—"

"Tish and pish, dear. Come on, the meat for dinner needs to sit for a few moments. We can have a look for those ration slips, hmmm?"

Sadie nodded, took a look outside before venturing in, the man beckoning her through the doorway like she was an itinerant aeroplane.

She took her shoes off, leaving them on the wooden hall floor, before taking a step into the living room. She audibly gasped. The place looked like it was straight out of one of the 'Best Home' magazines that her mum used to get. Back before the only important thing was boarding up the windows and doors.

Her feet sunk into the plush carpet, and she navigated a spindly coffee table, ambling dumbly towards an armchair. The man disappeared, and she heard the front door close. Staring down at the chair, she ran a hand down the back of her trouser legs; the last thing she wanted was to sully the pale cream chair with a smear of oil from climbing over the barricades at the end of the street.

She perched on the end of the cushion, unable to remember the last time she had felt this comfy. After a spot of cushion rearranging, she sat all the way back, allowing the chair to swaddle her skeletal frame with its padding.

The sound of slipper slapping on wood made her sit bolt upright. The man entered the room and saw her go to stand up. He raised a hand. "Now now, dear. Rest, relax, it's fine! You're a guest in our house, however temporary. Please, make yourself at home."

Sadie nodded and then reclined, surrendering to the elegant surroundings. She closed her eyes, thinking back to the old days, when her mum's house was kept as spick and span. Breathing in deeply, her brow furrowed and she opened her eyes. Her nose twitched. "What's that smell?"

The man smiled. "Ahhh, that's my dinner. Meat and two veg. Can't go wrong with meat and two veg."

Distant memories of Sunday roast dinners came flooding back. Sadie could feel her mouth fill with saliva. "Smells so good. What meat is that? Is it beef?"

The man nodded. "It most certainly is. I know someone who is a butcher. He always makes sure he keeps a prime piece of topside for me."

The sound of creaking floorboards from the room above interrupted Sadie's thoughts of meat dripping with gravy, piles of roast potatoes and a bonus Yorkshire pudding from her mum. "What's that upstairs?" she asked nervously.

Pointing to the ceiling, the man chuckled. "It's okay, dear. That's just my wife, Marjorie. She's just getting ready for dinner, I'd wager. Not quite as spritely on her feet these days unfortunately. She'll be fine. Now, let's go looking for those ration slips, hmmm?"

After the creaking, there came a scuffling sound. Slippered feet dragged across carpet, before another gentle thud. "I think she's found the dressing table. She'll just be putting her make-up on. Though she doesn't let on, she's got the hearing of a hawk. Must know we've got a guest; she's probably trying to look her best. Now I think I put them over…ah yes, here they are."

The man walked to the mantelpiece and picked up a wooden box, which had been sitting next to a gold plated carriage clock. Taking a seat on the sofa, the man opened the box and rooted through it, *ahhing* as he did so.

"Here we go, dear. How about these? Would they be any good for your little affected orphans?" the man asked. He held out a wad of yellowing paper slips, printed off centre. As Sadie took them, there came another thud from upstairs, louder. Some pottery or china fell off and tinkled as it broke on its descent. "Sounds like Majorie is having some trouble with her leg again. Go on dear, have a look through them, see if they're any good. My eyes aren't the best, I'm afraid. I'll be but a moment."

With that, the man stood up, placed the box on the table, making sure it was lined up perfectly with the table edge, and left the room.

As the sound of feet padding up the plastic covered stairs died down, Sadie flicked through the slips and started to pick out the children's ones.

In their haste, when the government began to issue the first batch of ration slips, it was a lottery which goods people would end up with. She remembered her neighbours ending up with everything but food chits. Luckily they all clubbed together, and managed to get through until the tier of bureaucracy, so often derided before the event, was reinstated, and managed to get the correct things out to the correct people.

"Did you have anyone affected?" the man asked. Sadie nearly jumped out of her skin. So preoccupied with sorting through the slips, she hadn't heard him come back into the room.

"Yeah…"

"Think everyone has, in some way or another. You should've seen this street when it all started. The Youngs, opposite us, with the green door? Ooohh, terrible business. She went first, got taken out by the postman. She heard a knock on the door. Before she even bothered to think, he had ripped her throat out. Marjorie saw it all, you know? She doesn't get round much, as I say, so she used to sit right there and watch.

"Their boy, Tommy I think his name was. He came out of the front door and saw her lying there with the postman over her. He was only a baby. Five, I think. Stood stock still with fear as his mother sat up. Didn't even try to run, Marjorie said. She grabbed hold of him and pulled his tongue out of his head.

"Mr Young had to take care of them, you know? His wife and his son. He used a shovel. It's still lying out there in the street. Got their blood all over it. Terrible business. Course, they were the first, but they weren't the last."

Sadie shifted uncomfortably in her seat. She waved the chunk of paper in the air. "I'll just take these then, if that's okay? Best be going really, you know? Get back home?"

The man, lost in his own world, chuckled, then looked up at her, his eyes unglazed. "Oh sorry dear, was miles away. Thinking back to those horrible days. Course, after a few weeks, we had to close all the curtains. Marjorie was a little annoyed. I know she was, but after those nasty men saw us and tried to break in…well, we had to do something, didn't we?"

"I think I should go now, sir," Sadie said again.

"Of course, of course! Unless…unless you want to stay for dinner? You'd be most welcome, you know. Got more than enough food prepared."

Sadie stood up; her bones ached as they adjusted to the lack of support. "No, thank you, really. I best be off. Thank you, though. It's a really nice gesture."

"Okay, dear," the man said. As he stood up, there was another crash from upstairs, and the man tutted. "Silly Marjorie…what's she knocked over this time?"

Edging towards the door, Sadie looked up at the artex ceiling, fearing that the old woman would fall clean through and ruin the picture-perfect room. "Is she alright? Sounded like a bit of a fall."

The man dusted himself down and ushered Sadie into the hallway. "She'll be fine. Always gets the odd nick and scrape these days. Age is a cruel mistress to us all; no regard for our achievements or valour."

As the pair walked down the hallway, there was yet another almighty crash. This time the man looked genuinely worried. "Oh my golly, I'm sorry. I better see to her quickly. Please, excuse me."

As the man trotted up the stairs, Sadie stood there for a moment. Should she stay? Should she go?

No, she had to get home.

She pulled level with the mirror, noticing the bags under her eyes. Taking a deep breath, she went to turn to the front door, but heard the beeping from the kitchen start again. Looking from the open kitchen door to the stairs, she went to shout, but just sighed. "Sod it, I'll do it myself." She walked down the hallway and into the kitchen. It was hard to believe that this room was even used.

The cupboards were all clean and shiny. The extractor fan whirred gently, free from grease. A pan bubbled softly on the hob. Standing in front of the cooker, she tried to work out the digital display, then gave up and started button mashing. This seemingly angered the beeping, made it more incessant. After another round of random pressing, it finally ceased. "Thank god for that," she muttered under her breath.

Taking a step back, she snuck a quick peek inside the oven. There was a roasting tray on the middle shelf, sizzling mounds of crisp roast potatoes arranged in neat rows. Sadie began to drool again; it had been so long since she had eaten something so lovingly prepared. The long days walking round the city left little time to prepare such lavish creations back home. Remembering she had to go, she turned to leave, walking straight into the man. "Sorry, dear," he said.

Sadie clamped a hand over her mouth.

"Did I frighten you dear? I'm sorry, I didn't mean to. I just wanted to come in and make sure you had worked the oven out okay. It's a bit temperamental, you see. Just like Marjorie." He laughed at some apparently secret joke.

"It's fine…just I didn't hear you," she said, trying to catch her breath.

Seeing her look across at the cooling meat, he pointed at it. "Would you like to take some home with you? We've got plenty. A steady stream of deliveries, right to our door as well!"

Looking at it, it struck Sadie that it seemed different from what she remembered. Bones jutted from one end, but they seemed thicker than they should be. "No, I'll be fine, thanks. Are you sure that's beef? It looks funny."

"What else would it be? Why don't you have a bit? See what it tastes like? It's all about the juices, you see. Got to make sure that the meat never gets dry. It goes down easier then, especially at our age. I'm lucky to have any proper teeth left. Marjorie on the other hand…well, she had hers whipped out a few years ago. Got dentures now, which are a bit awkward with some foodstuffs," the man replied.

"I'm sorry, forgot to ask. Is your wife okay?"

As if on cue, the sound of feet thudding on the stairs rang out. "Oh yes, dear. She had a spill, but she's a tough old girl. They don't make them like her anymore. Why don't you say hello before you go."

Sadie nodded and craned her head sideways. The sound grew louder as heavy feet plodded downwards.

A bony hand clutched the bottom of the bannister. A doleful moan echoed along the hall, Sadie gulped. "Hang on…I know that sound. *Everyone* knows that sound. She's…she's…"

"Yes, dear?" the man asked innocently.

Marjorie turned with the athleticism of an oil tanker and then she was standing in the hallway. She was dressed in a heavily blood-stained dress, a thin woolly cardigan hanging from her elbows. With her dentures missing, she slurped her gums together. Blackened bored out sockets looked right through the young woman. Her hands groped at the air, feeling for some support. Sadie held her hands over her mouth, trying to hold a scream inside.

"Doesn't she look a treat? Those nasty men who broke in here took her eyes, you see, but we took care of them with the rat poison. It's safer for me without her dentures, though of course, she can't infect me now anyway.

"So it is my solemn duty to feed her, keep her going, keep her strong. We made an oath you know! Till death us do part. Now, I must insist you stay for dinner. Though of course, you'll *be* the dinner. In a few days, when we've bled and seasoned your meat. You look rather succulent. Corn-fed, almost."

Sadie turned back to the old man, who was brandishing a shiny kitchen knife. He brought it across Sadie's throat, sending her to the floor, clutching the wound, which pulsed with blood.

As she lay dying on the floor, he stood over her. Droplets of blood pitter-pattered from the end of the knife onto her face. He leaned in closer. "Yes, you'll do very nicely."

GONE FISHIN'

The sun slumped on the horizon like an orange hill, its glow diffused by the early morning haze. The near still lake reflected the gently lilting clouds back up to the heavens.

In the middle of the water, a boat, graded barely above ramshackle in condition, bobbed as soft waves rolled under its hull. Lifting it gracefully skywards before depositing it smoothly onto the near glacial surface.

Two lines arched out from the vessel, like a wire frame rainbow puncturing the pristine veneer of Lake Shotbolt. A boy, still cranky after being woken from dreams of cricket and monsters, huffed once more, trying to get an ounce of attention from his father, who merely smiled to himself and continued to gaze out across the water.

With what he deemed subtlety expended, Cameron turned to his father and uttered the immortal line, "I'm bored."

Adrian laughed. "I knew it! How long have you been wanting to say that for?"

With his cheeks supported by balled fists, the child looked across. "Ages. Why do we have to come out fishing so early on a Saturday? You let Evie lie in! I could still be in bed or—"

"Playing Minecraft, yes, I know," Adrian sighed. He sat up, causing the boat to rock, breaking the neat perfect curvature of the fishing line from the water to boat. He waved an arm slowly across the vista in front of them. "Just look at this. I mean *really* look at it."

Trying his best, the kid huffed once more for good measure before leaning forward and resting his chin on the edge of the boat. Try as he might, he couldn't see the same thing as his father, and he gave up quickly. "There's nothing there, just the stupid lake, with the stupid forest, and the stupid dock."

Adrian sighed, leaning forward to join his son. He pointed out to the horizon, where the bulbous sun shimmered through a foggy gauze, and said, "Just look how beautiful it is. There's no one around, just you and me. Isn't that pretty special?"

The kid shrugged. "I guess, though we could still be at home."

Realising it was a losing battle, Adrian ruffled his son's hair. "One day, you'll see. Maybe you'll bring your kids down here and take them fishing too."

"Urrrggghh, I'm not having any kids," Cameron protested.

Adrian laughed and tugged gently on the fishing rod. Feeling nothing biting, he reclined in the boat once more, pulling his hat down to cover his eyes. "Guess they're all still sleeping."

"Sounds like they're the sensible ones," came the reply.

"Cheeky. I could always push you in, you know? See if any of the chompers are still in there?"

"Tell me again, Dad!"

Adrian smirked.

"Please?" Cameron begged, longing for something to take his mind off the tedium he was being forced to endure.

Tipping his hat up like an inquisitive cowboy, Adrian looked at his son. "You want to hear the story again? How many times have I told you already?"

"Hundreds! At least. Please…go on Dad, tell me how you and Mum got together."

Adrian opened his arm into a crook and nodded towards the created space. Cameron scampered across, plopped into the half-hug and looked up at his dad, as if he were an astronaut. "Fine," he conceded. "I'm glad you don't get bored of everything so easily."

Snuggling down together, the pair basked in the amber glow of the morning sun. Adrian squeezed Cameron gently before he began the well-weathered tale. "So, it was a day that started off very much like this one…"

Me, Bazza, Shane and Bret were out on a boat, a little bigger than this one, though it had no outboard. We always reasoned that the row out into the middle of the lake was on a par with any Sunday morning game of footie. It would either kill or cure the hangover from the night before, which seemed intent on trying to pop your eyes out of your head.

We'd gotten up late that morning. By the time we pushed off from the dock, there were already scores of people on jet skis buzzing up and down, slaloming in and out of the buoys. There was the odd brave soul swimming from the jetty over to Crazy Jerry's, at the edge of the forest over there. Everyone, well, *nearly* everyone, made sure they stayed clear of the Parasol Corp. building, over on the mouth of the river.

If the barbed wire fences weren't enough of a clue that they didn't want people snooping around, the men patrolling the perimeter with those snarling Alsations sure was. It was only the kids who dared otherwise, throwing themselves from the outflow pipes, pretending they were Olympic divers.

It was like the whole lake was alive with people, screaming, shouting, laughing, making the most of their Sunday, before normal life kicked back in the next day. We'd taken a few tinnies out. Nothing beats the after effects of the night before than a few cans the day after.

Don't worry, son, you'll know what I mean in a few years.

When we finally got to our usual spot, we cast our lines, sat back, and let the hubbub just wrap around us for a little bit. Bazza, as usual, was going on and on about this girl he'd met the night before, but then Bazza *always* did. It was like he had some kind of woman magnet sewn into his body.

Again, you'll care more about that in a few years too.

It was just another Sunday, nothing untoward.

Then, just as Shane chipped in about his bowling average that season, we all caught a whiff of something in the air. The lads went as quiet as anything. We were all looking around, trying to work out where it was coming from. It was a cross between exhaust fumes and rotting fish.

There were a few people out in the water actually gagging from the smell. One lad on a jet ski barfed as he whizzed by. It shot out, and sprayed all over his own face. It was disgusting. The guy pulled up to a halt a little way from us and was fishing bits of his brekkie out of his nostrils.

That set Bret off; he always had a weak stomach, began hurling over the side. I can just about stick the smell, but the sound is making my own guts gurgle like a blocked drain. I start to eye up the paper sack the beers were in as a spew bag, then we saw the kid bobbing around in the water.

He was face down. The waves had rolled him from the far side by the Parasol Corp. building, down towards the opposite shore. His back was covered in these red boils. Big huge bubbles ballooned before exploding in puffs of pus and wet skin. The body smacked into the side of our boat. Poor Bret didn't even see him, ended up vomming all over the kid's back.

I used an oar and bobbed the body under the water, so it washed the spew off. Bret and Shane each put an arm under an armpit and lifted him out of the water. He was dead, we all knew that. He'd been upside down for a good minute or so since we saw him. Who knows how long he'd been under?

We turned him over and, give him his dues, Bazza went to work. Pumped the water out of the kid's lungs, tried CPR, the works. No joy, unfortunately. The poor little blighter was gone.

Weirdly, every time Bazza sat up to take in another breath, that same rancid smell was coming out of the kid's mouth, like it was in him. We all looked at each other, and without having to say a word, went to reel in the lines and make our way back to shore. Then the damnedest thing happened. The boy opened his eyes.

Bazza was struck dumb. He taps me on the shoulder as I was going to start pulling in my line. I turn around, and when he finally regained the power of speech, he just mumbled, "Alive…" Which, considering what happened next, was odd.

I look down and saw that, yes, the kid does have his eyes and mouth open. I could also see that his hands were forming into little claws. I think I must've seen that before Bazza did.

I didn't even get a chance to say anything, as the little blighter leapt up and attached himself to Bazza's face like a leech. All of the background noise, including the bloke on the jet ski retching, just faded away. There was just the sound of Bazza punching this kiddie as it chewed on his cheek. It sounded like he was slapping a puddle.

Me and Bret were useless, just sitting there, gawping like teddy bears. Thank god Shane was on the ball. Though he could've warned Bazza about the oar. The kid must've wrestled him to one side just before impact. The oar cracked against the side of Bazza's face, taking off some of the kid's forehead.

Shane yelled at Bazza to stay still, before he managed to prise the oar under the kid's face, and scoop him off like he was a snail on a bit of decking.

So there we are, in the boat. In the middle of the lake. The four of us at one end, in danger of capsizing. The kid is sprawled out at the other, trying to disentangle his limbs from the bench and fishing line.

Shane didn't give him a chance. The kid lashed out, but ended up with the end of the paddle rammed right slap bang into the middle of his nose. There's this big crack as his face folds inwards, and then he fell slack. Black goo slopped out of the hole in his face. Looked like he had one huge nostril.

We start to relax a bit, which is good, as it stops us from tipping over. Shane pulled the end of the oar out of the kid's face, and prods the little blighter, seeing if he's still bitey. With the lull, Bret is finally able to start checking Bazza out.

"That's it," I said. "We're going back to shore, *now*." I pull on my fishing rod and reel it back in. Though straight away I can feel that I've got a bite. The tension on the line makes me forget everything, just for a few seconds.

Behind me, Bret is telling Bazza to take his t-shirt off and hold it to his face. I yank on the rod, determined to pull the first catch of the day out of the lake. In that moment, as it broke the surface, I saw that there was something very, very wrong with it.

There was a chunk missing from its back, and its face looked like it had been scoured with sand paper. It was heading right for me, its little mouth yapping away.

You know your dad, though. Got reflexes like a ninja.

So I duck, as the line and the fish fly over the top of me.

Poor old Bazza, though…well…he wasn't so lucky.

Now half naked, and with his favourite t-shirt soaking up blood from one face wound, he turns around just in time to see the most messed up fish in the world flap its tiny fins as it soared towards him. He screamed again as the fish clamped onto his other cheek. It was like a cartoon. This fish was sticking out from his face like a throwing star, still wriggling, its mouth chomping up and down on Bazza's cheek.

Well, that set him right off. He dropped his t-shirt and started pulling on the fish. In between bites, he managed to wrench it off his face, but once it was free, it thrashed around and bit down on Bazza's finger. It was like Pac Man. Starting at the tip, the fish began to chomp its way down. It got to the knuckle, which I thought might pose a problem, but it chewed straight through the bone. It was only when it got to the webbing bit that it stopped, as it couldn't open its mouth wide enough to start work on Bazza's hand.

Shane punched the fish in the gills and it finally gave up the ghost and slid along the bottom of the boat, coming to a rest against the dead kid. Now, we've all seen fish when you haul them out of the lake. They go into fitness overdrive, start doing press ups, their mouths flapping open and closed, trying to take in oxygen in order to keep on living.

This one, though? None of it. It just lay there, idly chewing on what was left of Bazza's finger. That was when Bret uttered the immortal line, "Strewth, mate, that's no ordinary fish. It's a bloody zombie fish!"

If we were in the pub when he'd said that, we would have started laughing. But when you've got a kid lying at one end of the boat with a hole in the middle of his face, Bazza looking like he's had a bomb go off in his mouth, blood shooting out of his index finger like an oil leak, and an undead fish trying to wriggle towards you across the hull…we figured he just might be right.

Shane cracked the end of the oar against the fish, making its guts spit out of its mouth and its eyes burst like bubble wrap. That god awful smell came out again, just amplified. With the paddle end, he scooped the remains up and hurled them back into the lake. After scraping the end of the paddle against the boat, he shoved it under the kid's body and lifted it into the water. Bret went to protest, but knew we were all better off with *it* in the water, than with it sitting opposite us, dead or not.

It was then that all three of us turned to look at Bazza. "What?" he asked. "Why are you looking at me like that?"

He knew, but he asked anyway, Bret pointed at the floating body and the direction of where the zombie fish had been thrown. "You've been bitten, mate…you could turn, become one of them."

Bazza, still bleeding out of his face and with one digit less than he'd had at the start of the day, sighed. "I don't want to be one of them, mate. I feel fine."

"Look at you! You're missing half your face. We don't know what's gonna happen, but if you turn mate…" Bret added.

Bazza turned to me as if I had the casting vote, and I just shrugged. Before I could say anything, Bazza threw himself into the water and began to swim ashore. It was a few hundred metres to the dock, and he was one helluva strong swimmer.

We all turned and saw where he went in, but couldn't see him at all. Then, like the majestic kraken, he burst through the surface like a man possessed. Turning towards the dock, he began to swim, putting everything he had into it, determined to get some help. Some real help, rather than his mates, who had decided it was safer to just cave his head in with an oar.

We were cheering him on, though. So was the jet ski barf guy, who pumped his fist in the air. I reckon he got about thirty metres, forty *tops*, before we saw the first of them. It leapt out from behind him, between his legs, slid down his back like a water chute, clamping on with its teeth at the base of his neck.

As he turned from side to side in the wash, the fish held on tightly, digging into the flesh even more. Bazza screamed, but he carried on, knowing that he just had to keep going, keep fighting. He could do it. We all knew it. Even as more of the fish began to bite into his arms and legs. Every stroke revealed more of the critters gnawing on his limbs.

Still he kept going.

Until about fifty metres out from shore, when he turned his head for air only for a giant zombified bream to broadside him and plunge into his open mouth. He thrashed around in the water, but he knew the truth. His race for life was done. As he vanished beneath the surface, all we saw was Bazza's ruined face, and the tail end of the zombie bream as it wriggled its way down his throat, into his guts.

We sat there for a moment in complete silence. Jet ski guy had sat down again, peeling bits of stomach lining from his face. He saw us and nodded respectfully, before a shoal of undead silver perch leapt out of the water and took him down. The jet ski rocked sideways. When it righted itself, the guy was gone, leaving nothing but a bloody smear on the seat.

Something broke inside of Bret at that moment. He snatched the oars and shouted, "THEY'RE ONLY BLOODY FISH MATE! C'MON, LET'S GET BACK TO SHORE, THEY CAN'T GET US THEN."

Like a man consumed by terror, he began to row back all by himself. Me and Shane fell backwards, caught off guard by his ferocity. I tried to lean forwards, get him to calm down. We were beginning to wheel to the left. Bret's face was a picture. The vein on the side of his head looked like it was going to burst through the flesh and throttle him.

He stopped and pulled the oar out of the water, yelling, "WHAT THE BLOODY HELL IS GOING ON HERE MATE?" As the paddle broke free from the lake, a longfin eel, which had huge gouges up and down its body, slid down the shaft and wrapped itself around Bret's arm. It was as if he were on fire. He stood up, flailing around. The eel began to stab its head into Bret's arm. Each time the snout lanced downwards, jets of blood flew out. Bret managed to get hold of the eel's head, but you could see in his eyes that he had gone beyond sanity.

He looked at the pair of us, and began to burble on about fish cakes and chips. Shoving the eel's head into his mouth, he bit it clean off, spitting the chunk of flesh overboard. As it plopped into the water, and began to sink, I could see its mouth still moving. Bret was still standing, though he had turned a putrid shade of green.

The eel unravelled like a length of rope and fell into the boat. Shane quickly picked it up and launched it over the side. Bret began to claw at his own face with his hands, revealing the bone beneath. Then he just stopped, looked at us and said, "Don't forget you'll need change for the bus ride home, fellas," before swan diving into the water.

He disappeared under like an anchor. We didn't even have time to try to grab him. Instinctively, I shoved my hand in the water, trying to snag him, only remembering in time about the issue with the undead sea life. I pulled my hand out as a rather large khaki grunter went to take it off at the wrist.

Me and Shane gawped at each other, both with the same look: the look of defeat.

What the hell could we do?

It was then that I heard her, your mum. That was when things started to change. I think for a moment beforehand, Shane thought about just pitching himself over the side too, letting himself get eaten alive by the zombie fish. Then her voice carried across the water.

Whereas everyone else was screaming as they were gnawed to death, or moaning as they reanimated and started eating other people, this one woman's voice was different. It was like an Amazonian warrior princess from hell. We both looked around, trying to work out where she was, if she was in danger. Though we should've known better. About a hundred metres away, bobbing around, holding onto a buoy, there she was.

In her free hand she held a length of chain, which she must've broken free from the buoy itself. As the zombie fish jumped out of the water, trying to bite her, or the eels tried to slip up from underneath where she was standing, she would batter the crap out of them.

Sorry. Language. I meant she would batter the hell out of them.

I think I fell in love right there and then. As she took out a trio of airborne rainbow fish with one mean backhand, she saw the pair of us, gawping right back. I can't repeat what she shouted at us, as it mainly consisted of swear words, but it definitely stirred us into life. Let's say that the polite version was, "Hey you two! Why don't you quit staring at me and come and get me, you pair of galahs."

We each took a side of the boat, plunged the oars into the water and rowed for our lives. There were times we knew that the zombie fish were onto us, but we just kept going. After all, if she could hold them off single handed, then we sure as hell could row a boat over to her.

Despite feeling like we were stuck in tar, from all the zombie fish trying to clog us up from underneath, we were making good progress. Even when rogue-spotted-flagtail began to leap out of the water and dive bomb us, trying to nibble our flesh, we fought our way to her. A few times one of us yelped as tiny fish teeth chewed on our shorts, or slapped against the bottom of the boat and tried to flap their way to us.

Eventually, we made it to her. With the chain wrapped around her fist, your mum punched a rogue bream in the face and leapt into the boat. As soon as she landed, me and Shane pushed away, trying to get some distance from the zombie eels that were already winding their way around the buoy.

Taking a well-earned break, we made our introductions. "I'm…erm…Adrian," I finally mustered, making her smile. Your mum has got the best smile, huh? She looked at me, my heart beating in my throat, and she said, "Lisa. Pleased to meet ya," before she backhanded a flying perch back into the water.

Shane, ever the tactful one, asked her, "I'm Shane. Before we go any further though, Lisa, one pertinent question. Why the hell are you out here holding onto a buoy?"

Your mum shot him a look. You know the one. Then she pointed at the blood-stained jet ski. Again, I'll give you the clean version. "That flamin' drongo ditched me when it all kicked off."

Satisfied, Shane managed to mumble a proper hello, before adding, "Do you know what's going on, Lisa? Why have all the fish turned into zombies? Is there no more room in fishy hell, do ya reckon?"

She laughed, then pointed to the effluent pipes from the Parasol Corp. chemical plant. "I think it might have something to do with that, don't you?"

For the first time since it had all began, we looked across to the imposing factory, and saw luminescent green goo being pumped into the usually pristine clear lake. "Ahh yeah, guess that would do it," Shane replied.

"What the hell are we going to do?" I asked.

Your mum, as you know, has an answer for everything, whether we want to hear it or not, or even if she's right or wrong. She pointed to a jetty, used by the jet skis and powerboats. "See that over there? We need to get some of those fuel drums. Reckon we could blow the pipes up, stop the goo from coming out. Least then we can start to contain it."

Couldn't really argue with her logic, so we pointed the boat towards the jetty and began the journey. It was as if the zombie fish knew what we were doing. A surge of them ran under the hull, trying to flip us all out into the water and into their bellies. As me and Shane put everything into the rowing, your mum lashed the chain under the boat, trying to stop the fish from converging too much in one place.

As we got near to the fuel, Shane screamed as a hand, with most of the skin already ripped off, broke through the water and grabbed hold of the side of the boat. It tried to capsize us once more, but your mum wasn't having any of it. She ran the chain under the bony wrist, looped one end over the other and pulled it taut, slicing the hand off like it was a piece of cheese. With a flurry of bubbles, the zombie person sank under the waves.

When we got to within a few feet of the jetty, your mum jumped across and tied the boat to a post. Me and Shane clambered over each other to get off. I've never been so happy to get out of a fishing boat, I tell ya now, son.

After he caught his breath, Shane took one look at us then across at a jet skier, who was being chased around the lake by a shoal of frenzied zombie fish, and legged it.

I don't blame him. Even now when we see him in the pub, we say hello. A man can only see so much death, destruction, and zombified perch, before they go insane. Your mum called him something rude, though, which was fair enough.

Between the pair of us, we rolled two drums into the boat, before I came up with a bonzer idea. There was one jet ski left. Having dropped the drums off, and picking up a convenient flare gun from an emergency box, I tied the rope from the boat to the jet ski. Like a cowboy, I mounted the jet ski and motioned for your mum to join me. She was a little reluctant at first, but she could see that I was the kind of guy who would finish what he started.

No sooner had I fired up the engine than the damn fish were back, trying to nibble at our feet, flinging themselves into our laps. Your mum wrapped one arm around me and began to swing the chain around our bodies like it were nunchucks. Gunning the engine, I started to blaze a trail to the outflow pipe.

Having seen what had happened to the others, I made sure that I obeyed the five D's of jet ski piloting whilst being chased by undead fish; dodge, duck, dip, dive and dodge again.

As we got nearer the pipe, I squeezed your mum's hand, and she swivelled on her seat, ready. With the jet ski slowing down, the boat caught us up, and she jumped into the back. With a strength her body belied, she deadlifted one of the drums and braced for action.

With some rather excellent driving by me, your mum shoved the barrel into the pipe, which, fortunately, was a perfect fit. The oozing slowed down to a trickle, though there was a low bassy grumbling from the pipes as the pressure began to build.

Your mum clambered back on board the jet ski and hugged me once more, this time with both hands. I revved the engine and burst away, ready to get to a safe distance so we could blow it up and get off the lake.

Then, beneath the water, there was a deep rumbling. It was all around us, as if the very lake was turning against us. I gunned the motor and fought to outrun the tremor. As a huge WHOOSH sounded from behind us, I brought us round in a one-eighty skid, so that we faced the way we had just come.

You've probably heard the story of the Great Kath Hoolu; the giant octopus that lives at the bottom of Lake Shotbolt. So called because its first victims were Mr and Mrs Hoolu, from Tazmania. Kath survived the encounter, though her husband wasn't so lucky. Poor old Kath didn't speak to too many people after, though. Mad as a box of tofu salami, by all accounts. Hardly surprising.

Anyway, every few years or so, stories would circulate about it waking from its slumber, and how it would feast on anything foolish enough to be on the water at the time.

Of course, we all thought it was a myth, told by our parents to scare the hell out of us. I remember your grandad used to tell me that the Great Kath Hoolu would crush me in my sleep if I didn't eat my greens.

But, clear as day, there it was, the giant zombified octopus, Great Kath Hoolu itself. There were bits of its body hanging off, like it had been chewed on or melted. Its head was pulsating, like a day-glo water balloon being filled. Every time it throbbed, fish would throw themselves at us from the inky depths.

Right then, me and your mum looked at each other, knowing what the hell was going on. This zombie octopus was telepathically controlling the undead fish. If we could stop it, then maybe, just maybe, we could stop all of the others.

I must admit, I was staring at your mum a bit too long, which very nearly cost me my life. A huge tentacle shot out from the water, just missing my head by a matter of inches. I got my head back in the game. Your mum knew what to do, and she jumped back into the boat once more.

I pulled on the throttle and set off across the lake, turning violently from side to side, trying to avoid getting clobbered by the giant tentacles. One of them swished right across my face. I could make out the huge suckers on the bottom, the size of dinner plates.

I swung to a halt and nodded to your mum. It would have to be on this pass. She grabbed hold of the barrel like it weighed nothing at all and wedged her feet under the boat seats, as if it were a giant snowboard. Even when I went to full power, she wasn't affected in the slightest, expertly guiding the boat like a champion boarder.

Pulling in close to the Great Kath Hoolu, I looked into one of its baleful eyes. I swear I saw some fierce evil intelligence within. Your mum tossed the fuel drum at its head, which it instinctively caught with one of its tentacles.

We came to a halt and I pulled out the flare gun, but then I froze. We only had one flare, locked and loaded. Which do we go for?

The drum in the monster's grip?

Or the one rammed in the pipe?

Your mum jumped out of the boat, onto the back of the jet ski, and not a moment too soon as a tentacled arm came down and smashed the boat into kindling. My decision was made. Aiming at the fuel drum being investigated by the beast, I stood up on the running board, gave your mum a cheeky wink, and said, "Blow me," to the zombie octopus, and pulled the trigger.

The flare corkscrewed through the air in slow motion, before slamming into the drum. For the briefest of moments, I swear that I saw the Great Kath Hoolu raise an eyebrow in shock, unable to comprehend its impending destruction.

Time flickered back to normal speed, and a huge fireball erupted, tearing the fiend apart, sending giant size pieces of calamari into the air, which showered the little café on the shore.

Sitting back down again, I blew a wisp of smoke from the gun barrel and gave your mum a high five. All around us, dead fish bobbed to the surface of the water, all decayed and withered. As we headed back to the dock, we heard a squeaking from behind us.

Daring to look, we saw the pipe explode in a shower of green slime, causing a chain reaction to ripple down the infrastructure, to the chemical plant itself, which went up in a pyrotechnic display that would've made Michael Bay moist.

With the burning backdrop behind us, and your mum hugged up behind me, I lit a cigar and we made our way back to shore, the Great Kath Hoolu, its zombie fish horde and Parasol Corp. defeated.

Adrian looked down to see his son sleeping on his chest. He ruffled his hair and looked to the horizon. One of the fishing lines began to twitch.

Gently resting Cameron on the boat seat, Adrian began to reel it in. It was a big 'un, putting up a helluva fight. It had taken a while for the fish to come back to this blighted place, but maybe, just maybe, this would be the biggest catch of the year.

With the line right by the boat, Adrian took a moment to rest. Taking a deep breath, he heaved the catch out of the water. The hook was sticking through a nostril, having threaded itself through the upper jaw bone.

Adrian looked down to see that the torso it was attached to ended at the waist. As languid jaws snapped at him in mid-air, Adrian smiled. "Alright, Bazza. I was just talking about you, mate."

WHACKOS

<static squall>

—reports of further firestorms over Calais are still coming in. Eyewitnesses have told us that they've seen evacuation boats adrift and ablaze in the channel. It would seem that any further attempts to get people out of the docks there are going to have to wait until the fires have burned themselves out.

Weather now. It will remain cool overnight, with the odd showery outburst. A high of nineteen degrees tomorrow, staying clear and dry.

Now, at seven o'clock in the evening, it's time to pass over to Slim Chuckney for his weekly show, 'Get The Skinny', where he takes a look at the stories behind the apocalypse.

One-oh-two-point-nine-FM

This is Radio Freedom, broadcasting to you across the country.

Through trial and adversity…comes freedom.

Good evening, and welcome to another edition of Get The Skinny, with me, your host and intrepid reporter, Slim Chuckney. Since society was reclaimed from the walking dead, some ten months ago now, we here at Get The Skinny, have strived to bring you death-defying reports from what very nearly was the end of the world.

This week, though, we're doing something a little different.

In the main, we, and every other syndicated investigative news show, have focussed on those who were front and centre when the fight to take back our world started, and ended. We've looked at the generals, the soldiers on the streets of our cities, towns and villages. We've spoken to politicians, doctors, and teachers, each with their own story to tell.

But tonight, ladies and gentlemen, we are going to shine a light on the unsung heroes of what is happening right now, up and down this country, in your very street.

You've probably seen them, driving around in their black transit vans, with their breathing masks and high-vis yellow jackets. Officially, their title is, 'Welfare Acclimatisation Care Operative', yet, on the rubbish strewn streets, they've earned nicknames such as body-packers, life-sweepers and, more cruelly, whackos. An unfortunate take on the acronym of their work.

Although the soldiers and paramilitary forces may have cleared many off the streets, these fearless men and woman are tasked with going into the many thousands of abandoned houses, dealing with the effects of three years' worth of neglect.

Every day, they tackle, head on, the past that many have forgotten. And, all too often, they come face to face with the ghouls who came so close to wiping humanity out.

After much wrangling, myself and trusty recording engineer, Rich Hawkins, were able to get access to a ride along, spending a few hours with one such pair of workers. Tonight, we bring you an exclusive look at the true cost of the fight against the undead.

The human cost.

Warning to anyone of a sensitive nature, there are things contained within this report which may trigger flashbacks to those dark days. We recommend anyone who suffers from these, or is of a weak disposition, to turn the volume down on your radio, now.

As usual, there is strong language and opinions throughout.

Slim Chuckney (SC): This is just another normal street. Back before the dead started walking, there would have been mothers pushing prams along this tarmac. Children running down it, zipping in between people to get to the park, whilst commuters would trudge to their jobs, pining for the return journey. Home. Yet today, things are oh so different.

Communities are still struggling to get back to a sense of normality. Though the residents are starting to move back in, the true price we have paid, in human life, is only now becoming apparent. Displaced survivors must apply to their councils to move back into the shells they once called homes. When enough residents have signed up, teams of Welfare Acclimatisation Care Operatives descend on these overgrown lanes, ready to make them habitable once more.

Of course, though, behind some of the doors, those who opted to stay still remain. Both those that lived through it all, feeling safer in familiar surroundings, eking out an existence, and…those who didn't. The victims of the plague that ravaged our world. Their stories are locked away, like a time capsule.

The task of making the streets and houses of every population centre in the cleared zones safe again falls to these workers. Two of whom I have the privilege of spending the day with today. Morning guys, could you just tell our listeners your names please?

Daryl Duncan (DD): I'm Daryl, and can we get a fucking move on please? Got enough to do today as it is.

Adam Millard (AM): Hello! I'm Adam, and you just ignore this grumpy bear, he'll be fine once he gets his morning coffee. Come on, Mister Grizzly. Have this, and I'll go see what's behind door number one.

SC: Thanks, Adam. So, could you tell us what your average day consists of?

AM: Sure thing Slim. It is Slim, right?

SC: It sure is.

AM: Not short for anything is it?

SC: Like what?

AM: I dunno, Slimanie? Slimathy?

SC: Nope, just Slim. Short for Slim. So, Adam, what does a standard day as a Welfare Acclimatisation Care Operative look like?

AM: Well, we clock in at the depot, and our super gives us a list of houses we have received rehoming permits for. Now, it's all well and good moving Mr and Mrs I'm-Still-Alive back into their two up, two down, as the likelihood is that, elbow grease aside, it'll be clear. The problem we have is that we are required by law…statute Z seventeen, sub section twelve, if you want to know, to clear the houses neighbouring them.

SC: Why is that?

AM: When we first started, we'd go right ahead and clear out the house that was assigned for rehoming. Then, a few days, or in some cases *hours*, later, we'd get a message slip from the courier, that there were 'strange noises' coming from the houses next door.

SC: And that's from the zombies, right?

AM: Bingo! Say, you're a smart cookie aren't ya, Slim? So, the powers that be said that we had to clear the houses neighbouring the one we were doing. I'm guessing those folks didn't really want to listen to the dead moaning at all hours. That it kinda upset them.

The last thing we want is hurt feelings, eh, Slim?

SC: Sure thing. These folk have been through a lot. I spoke to this one family, who were living in a tree house for nigh on—

AM: I was being sarcastic, Slim. Did you not detect my tone?

SC: Erm, no? Sorry…

DD: Are you two dildos still standing out here? Come on, I've got the invite. Let's get cracking with the knacking.

SC: Is that an axe in your hand?

DD: No darling, I'm just pleased to see ya. Come on, three houses in one day is pushing it. Let's get going.

AM: See what I mean? He perks up later in the day, you'll see.

<sound of axe smashing through wood>

SC: Don't you have keys? Or some kind of lock-picking kit? This is someone's house, you know?

DD: Excuse me, Mister Fancypants. Do you think that at the start of the apocalypse, every tenant passed a copy of their front door key to the council, for just such an occasion? Look here, Slim, if that is even your real name, you're not here because we want you to be, so how about a bit of hush now whilst we do some real work, huh?

SC: But it makes so much noise.

AM: Which is part of the process. Look, we've got spare doors in the wagon. Once we've done our thing, we just put a new one on. People like that, it makes them feel like they've got a brand spanking new house. Plus, it helps for one other thing…

<sound of axe smashing through wood>

SC: I can't—

<sound of moaning echoing down the hallway>

SC: SHIT! LET'S GET OUT OF HERE.

DD: Woah there, Ross Kemp, not so fast. Ad, you got yours handy?

AM: Sure do, cocked and locked.

SC: Is that…is that a gun?

DD: What do you think it is, a bunch of grapes? Course it's a fucking gun. Do you know how many houses we open up have at least one dead fuck inside them?

SC: No…is it a lot?

AM: Around one in three, my little jar of strawberry jam. See the axe comes in handy so we can get in quickly, and alerts any of those pesky zombies inside to our presence. Oooohhhh, look, here's one now. Daryl, doesn't he look a bit like Benny?

DD: Ha, you're right! He does. Dead spit, so he is.

SC: I'm sorry, was Benny a friend of yours?

AM: No, he looks like Benny Hill. Oh this will be a good one.

<gunshot>

DD: You fucking idiot, you winged him. I swear, you shoot like my wife.

SC: What? Badly?

DD: Of course badly, she's fucking dead, isn't she. Hit it again, you nonce. Quit fucking about, I gotta curl one out soon.

<gunshot>

<gunshot>

AM: There, his milk cart racing days are most certainly over.

DD: WATCH OUT!

<dull sound of axe>

DD: You were lucky there, my man. Never go into a house without giving it a wee minute to calm down. Never know where these dead fucks are hiding.

SC: Th..t…thank you…do they always twitch like that?

AM: Only the horny ones. Give me the axe, Daryl, and I'll get the sheeting from the wagon.

DD: You alright, my man? Not gonna be sick are ya?

SC: I'm fine…I've seen a dead body before, you know.

DD: For sure, just these ones tend to be a little ripe, know what I'm saying?

SC: So what happens now?

DD: Well, Ad will cover the doorway in this thick plastic sheet. Fits over it just so. Stops people walking by looking in and seeing the mess, cos hey, everyone's so fucking sensitive these days eh?

You'd think after the dead fuck apocalypse that people would be a bit more hardened, but that's just how it is. Plus, the sheet sticks to the doorframe, as the last thing you want is anyone to get out. Especially if they've got no legs, or one of them bites us, and we turn.

SC: Good thinking.

DD: I don't make the fucking rules. If I had my way, I'd have a fucking flamethrower. Be done with it proper like. Oh Skinny, before you go in, you'll probably need this mask.

SC: But you're not wearing one?

DD: The smell of those rotting brains is making you and your man's nose twitch like a cat's arse at the vets. We're around this seven days a week; we've become somewhat immune to it. Adam here uses it as aftershave, eh?

AM: Damn right I do. Gets the ladies quivering at the knees.

DD: Ladies? But I thought you were…never mind. Look, take the mask or don't bother, no skin off my nose. Just if you empty your guts in there, we ain't cleaning it up.

Rich Hawkins (RH): I think I'll take one of those…

AM: Right, let's get in there and see what we've got. You lot go first, I'll secure the entrance behind us.

SC: My…even through the mask you can smell it. It reminds me when we evacuated through the sewers, right beneath the feet of the undead. It just permeates everything. It's making my eyes sting.

Hey, Rich, look at this. All these letters are from a few days before the announcement was made that the fightback had failed. No way! Even a copy of the Times, with the immortal headline, 'THE DEAD HAVE SEEN THE END OF WAR'. This is a collector's item.

What's through here? Ahh, it's the living room. It's absolutely filthy. My god…is that…is that?

DD: Sure is, Skinny. I'd wager some early looters got the fright of their lives when they came in here. Don't think Mr and Mrs Dead-Fuck gave them a chance to come back. Must've eaten them in a few sittings. This is all that's left of them.

SC: They tore through their tracksuits as if it were tissue paper.

DD: Aye, and the rats probably. Mind you, the teeth marks on the ribs look a little odd.

SC: This place just seems so…so weird, strange, like they just upped and left. Gone away on a long cruise and let the place just go to rack and ruin. What do you guys do in here now?

AM: Anything which is rotten goes. Any personal effects. So those bills in the hallway, clothes, towels, you name it, none of it is any cop now, it all goes in the bin. Then we'll check the electrical equipment, but most of that will go too. Anything battery operated will be next to useless, and most other gear won't work anymore. If by any miracle it does, we'll take it back to the depot, where it gets 'redistributed'.

DD: Which is a polite way of saying that someone higher up the food chain gets some nice stuff, know what I'm saying?

SC: Okay, so there have been a number of reports from people saying that you guys are nothing more than tomb raiders. What do you have to say about those rumours?

DD: Who said that?

SC: You know, whispers round the campfires, chit chat at the bar.

AM: You spend much time round a campfire, Slim?

DD: Hey, that's okay. I can answer your question. We're not thieves, Skinny, of that I can assure you.

SC: So nothing goes missing when you go through people's homes.

DD: If you want to know if we're thieves, you just have to ask. Straight out, like a man.

SC: …

AM: Here it comes, Daryl. Look at that face. Either that or he's had too much powdered cheese and he's constipated.

SC: Okay, fine, I'll ask. Do you steal from people's houses?

DD: BOOM! There we have it. Good man. Takes balls to ask the proper questions. If you want to know anything, Slim, please do. As opposed to those people who have come out of their bunkers and back into their gilded cages, we appreciate a bit of direct questioning, ya know?

SC: Fine, good, so, are you?

DD: No, we're not. Well, as far as I know, me and Adam aren't. We don't know what the others get up to. I'd say, much like people in general, that there are some bad eggs.

SC: But this is people's lives you're sifting through. Deciding what to throw away and what stays. That's a pretty powerful position to be in. You're rifling through their photo albums, throwing away their life, their very history.

DD: Aye, for sure, and it's a job we don't take lightly either. Answer me something, Slim, who lived here?

SC: Eh?

DD: Who lived here, before the world went to shit? What were their names?

SC: I…errr…don't know. How would I know?

DD: You looked through their mail didn't ya?

SC: Yeah, but…

DD: James and Tricia Jobling.

SC: Sorry?

DD: That was their names, and judging by this here picture, I'd say that they are the ones lying out in the hallway with their heads smashed in and their toes curling up, wouldn't you say?

SC: How di—

DD: Before we do a job, Slim, we take a few moments to find out who lived here beforehand. Small things like knowing how many there were.

Do you know how many people in this country survived this? Give or take.

SC: Estimates are around two million, difficult to say.

DD: Exactly, that means that around fifty eight million people are dead, in one way or another. We need to know, or at least have an idea, of who lived in this building before we go into it. Not because we want to know if they looked rich, or if they have much to steal, but to get an idea of who they were. In many cases, we are emptying out dead people's homes. Their possessions will never get claimed or looked through. Here look, the photos are fucked, wrecked by three years of the elements blowing their shit in here and ruining them.

What if they had survived?

They come back in here and find the place like this, do you think that would be easy for them? Having given up on the hope of ever setting foot back in here again only to find that the one thing that kept them going had all gone to shit.

That is why we do what we do. It's why people aren't allowed to come back until we've been around. We are the motherfucking detergent, you know? We come in, clean the place up of any trace of the horror that has gone on here. Most places that were abandoned were broken into, either by survivors, looters or the dead fucks. All those lives are trodden into the carpet, sprayed up the walls, saturated into their curtains.

We take out everything that is broken, and leave anything that is of use. Some of these photos will remain, but they will stay in a government-issued drawer, in a government-issued cabinet. Pretty much all of this furniture will go on the pyre. Once we're done here, the stackers come in and put in the replacement government-issued beds, mattresses, fucking oven, the basics that people need.

Not in case Mr and Mrs Jobling come back, cos they're dead and leaking congealed blood over the floor, which we're gonna have to strip and burn I might add. We're not doing it for them, we're doing it for those that come after them. The refugees that even now, flood in from Europe, some even from America. Those places where the infection still ravages without care or mind. So that when Mr and Mrs fucking Schmidt come in here, to make this their home, even if it is temporary, they have an idea of the people who came before them.

Of those who didn't make it. Through these scant fucking offerings, we keep James and Tricia alive. So, no, Slim, me and Adam aren't thieves. We're just men who need to be kept busy, because the consequences of being idle are too much to even fucking contemplate.

SC: Wow, man, that is just so…so…so evocative, you know? Thanks for sharing, Daryl.

DD: No bother. Now, if you've managed to hold your breakfast in so far, I've got something which will really test your constitution. Come on.

Adam, you gonna be alright finishing up in here?

AM: Sure thing, mate. Most of this is gonna have to go. I'll pull the soft furnishings down, and clean the windows up. I'll give you a shout when I'm ready to do upstairs.

DD: Good man. Come on, Slim, Rich, have I got smells to introduce to you.

SC: Say, Daryl, what do you say about people that call you whackos?

DD: That's pretty funny. They got that from Welfare Acclimatisation Care Operative huh?

SC: Sure did. Do you think it's demeaning at all?

DD: You've seen a little bit of what we have to do, Slim. I'd think you'd agree that in order to do it, and not blow your brains out at the end of the day, you have to be a little bit out there.

SC: I guess, but don't you think calling you a whacko is a little mean-spirited?

DD: Boo-fucking-hoo, there it is again. Why should I care about what other people think of me? While they're there bitching about what we're doing, what exactly are they up to? Nah, fuck 'em. Do you know what I was doing when the clean-up teams found me, about a year ago?

SC: No, what were you up to?

DD: I was living in a chest freezer at the edge of a quarry. At first they thought *I* was a fucking zombie. I was covered in shit, dried blood down my face from where I kept banging my head on the freezer-catch, which I had to jimmy open. One of the militia was about to ventilate my head, then I asked them if they had any Guinness. Don't know who shit themselves first; me, when I realised I was stark-bollock naked, or my man who was about to pull the trigger.

Point is, least I think there's a point to this little fable, I was pretty fucking far out, ya know? When they cleaned me up, and I had a few smokes, I felt bad, wanted to do something. Plus, when you've spent nigh on three years hanging onto life by your fucking fingernails, the thought of sitting around waiting for someone else to bring you something…well…it just didn't sit right. Soon as I found out about the WACO jobs, I jumped at the chance.

Watch out Rich, you don't want to…aww mate, no it's fine, you'll be able to scrape those bits of manky brain off your boots later. Just try not to walk it round too much. Wipe it on his shirt. Good man. So, anyway, you guys ready? Get a load of this.

SC: What…wh…what the hell is that smell?

<sound of dry retching>

RH: It smells so bleak…

DD: Ha ha ha ha ha, you should see your faces, it's hilarious. See, I've gotten used to the aroma. Most I don't even realise nowadays, but kitchens are always the worst. You've got all that rotten food, which has pretty much dissolved away to nothing, but in the process it's helped all kinds of funky shit to grow. Hey boys, come here, the fridge is always a right treat.

<continuous sound of dry retching>

RH: My eyes! Hang on…what cheese is that?

SC: That's not cheese, Rich.

DD: If you two weren't here, I wouldn't have even bothered to open this. We just tape them shut and bin them. You should've seen Adam when we opened the first one. I thought he was gonna spew out of his arse, it was that bad.

SC: Would you mind closing it please? Thanks

RH: I'm not sure I will ever be able to smell anything again.

DD: You'll be fine, Rich. Give it a few days.

SC: So, Daryl, where's your home? Do you worry what you'll get back to?

DD: I know what I'll get back to: charred fucking rubble. I'm from Ballymena. You probably heard what they did, yeah?

SC: I sure did. It sounded pretty horrific.

DD: That's a fucking understatement. Used it as a little test case, so they did. Firebombed the entire town, thought they'd be able to flush the dead fucks out. Do you know all they achieved?

SC: No, what did they do?

DD: They managed to make it the easiest fucking follow-up census in the history of mankind. You could count the survivors on a pair of hands. I made it back to my house, least I think it was my house. Pretty difficult to tell, as anything metal had melted, and the houses and streets had bubbled from the heat.

Tried to find my family. I had only escaped what happened because I was pissed, but they never even had a warning. All I could find was a stain on the wall, which kind of looked like my wife, though it could've just been a chair, you know?

SC: I'm so sorry, Daryl, really I am.

DD: Thanks, my man. I was hurting for ages after that, then one day, when I was sitting in that chest freezer, it hit me. Would they have survived everything I had been through up until that point? Was being burned alive in a flash a better way to go than being eaten by the dead fucks, or worse, coming back as one?

SC: I…don't know…what do you think?

DD: I think that in order for me to wake up each day, I have to believe that what happened probably spared them, and me, from a far worse fate. Doesn't stop me missing them, though, not by a long shot.

SC: SHIT! What's that over there? In the corner! Those bones, is it a baby? A child? Looks like a small skeleton.

DD: That? That's not a baby. Look at the skull, it's a fucking dog. Well…was. Now it's just a jumble of bone. Ahhh, course.

SC: What?

DD: That explains the bite marks on the ribs we saw in the living room.

SC: Are you saying that the dog *ate* the people?

DD: Don't be daft man. The dogs tucked into the bodies after the fuckheads killed them, before they turned.

SC: So the dogs were alive when the…when James and Tricia turned?

DD: Well yeah.

SC: But there's been no recorded sightings of the dead eating animals, so how did they die?

DD: True, they might not eat them, but they don't exactly feed them either, do they?

SC: Eh?

DD: Look, do you know what type of dead bodies we find more of, even more than humans?

SC: Dogs?

DD: Yep, and cats. Fuck me, guinea pigs, hamsters, gerbils, cock-a-fucking-tiels. Hell, even goldfish bones resting on those weird stones at the bottom of dried up fishbowls. When the dead started walking around again, and eating people, or people turned after infection, most pets were still indoors. Do you know how long it takes to starve to death?

After a week or so of not eating, a dead body here or there will start to look pretty damn appealing. Now we know that they don't eat the dead fucks, cos…well…why would you? Only carrion would.

I saw a crow once eating one of their brains.

RH: Shut up, that's a lie.

DD: Straight up. Was walking down the road, his head was all busted open, like someone had got busy with an axe, you know? Anyway, this big fuck-off crow was sitting on the cracked open bit of skull, pecking away at what was left inside. This dead fuck didn't even know it was there; just veered on down the road, oblivious to everything.

So anyway, I'd say Mr and Mrs Jobling got infected early on. Must've been one of the easily susceptible, or one was, and bit the other. Either way, they both popped their clogs. You get a couple of jokers breaking in the first week or so, bit off more than they could chew, *literally*. The Joblings have their fill and leave the bodies. Next thing you know, Fido comes along, has a whiff and thinks, 'Well it's not exactly Pedigree fucking Chum, but it's better than nothing'. Ate enough so they couldn't come back, probably had enough to tide him over for a bit, then the inevitable happened and he carked it.

Poor little fella.

Mind you, when I tell Adam about this, he'll make us bury him in the garden. He's a big dog lover.

SC: That's so nice.

DD: Yeah, but he can't eat a whole one.

SC: What? He…eats dog?

DD: Ha ha ha ha, course not, you idiot, just winding you up. For a reporter, you seem a bit gullible. Tell me Slim, what did you do when the world went to shit?

SC: I was a lecturer, at a University.

DD: And how did you survive?

SC: Me and my family made it to the commune in Savernake forest. We holed up there through the worst of it, before the New Cavaliers came through, burning the place down, killing folk. Then we got out of there and went north, lived off the land until a patrol found us.

DD: Ahhh, I've heard of you lot. They called you Ewoks, didn't they?

SC: May have done…

RH: Ewok? Sounds about right.

DD: How about you, Rich?

RH: Well, I'm from Somerset.

DD: So, you fucked your brother through the entire three years?

RH: No, actually, we're not a bunch of inbred yokels, you know.

DD: Didn't say a word, Rich. You gotta stay warm somehow; what better place than an extended stay at the Incest Hotel?

RH: If you must know, our knowledge of the land and seasons helped us deal with the whole survival thing very well, actually.

DD: I reckon the extra fingers and webbed toes came in handy too?

RH: Look here mate, I—

DD: Calm down Rich, I'm just messing. I read the reports, you know. I saw that the highest survival rates came from the countryside. You lot were the only ones who knew how to live without electricity, got back to basics in no time.

RH: Yeah, well…you know…it wasn't easy, but we made it.

SC: So, Daryl, how about you? What did you do before the world ended?

DD: Me? I was a musician, travelled round as a session guitar player, appeared on a few albums, ya know? Though I was always happiest when I was playing in my own band, down our local.

SC: What was it called?

DD: The Slug and Puddle.

SC: Nooo, the band.

DD: Ah right, we were called, Funky Murder Disco.

<sound of laughter>

SC: Okay…what sort of music did you play?

DD: It was a sort of rock/pop/country/synth combo. You say it out loud and it sounds like we must've been shit…and we were, but we didn't care. We played because it made us happy, you know? Life is too short, you gotta do what you enjoy, else you wake up one morning and everything you had is fucking gone. You gotta feel like you gave it your all. What else is there?

AM: Tell him your theory.

SC: You scared the hell out of me then.

AM: Sorry mate. Go on, Daryl, tell him your theory. You know, about what happened?

DD: Fuck you, Adam.

SC: What's this?

AM: Daryl has his own theory on how the dead started walking. Go on, tell him.

DD: Hey, Adam, there's a dead dog over by the bins.

AM: Aww no, where's my burial shovel?

SC: What's your theory, Daryl?

DD: Yous two are just gonna fucking laugh and ridicule me.

SC: A lively debate is the heart of any friendship.

DD: Is that what we are now, Slim? Friends?

SC: You know what I mean. Come on, spill.

AM: This is a corker.

DD: Okay, fine. Here goes. Do you remember about a year before it all kicked off, that instead of smoking, people were using those vape…things, E-Cigs, whatever you want to call 'em?

SC: Yeah, had a few friends use them to give up smoking.

DD: Anyway, I call them dickhead-flutes, cos at the end of every one of them is a fucking hipster dickhead. Don't you think it's a bit convenient how they start smoking them, and then a few months later, the world is overrun by zombies?

SC: Erm…

RH: Ha ha ha, and you called me stupid.

DD: No, Rich, I didn't call you stupid. I insinuated that you were an inbred mutant hick, there's a big difference.

SC: But the outbreak has been proven to be some kind of hybrid infection.

DD: Proven by who?

SC: Well…the scientific community for one.

DD: The same scientific community that said that these dickhead-flutes posed no hazard to anyone? Please. If you can't see that this is a huge conspiracy, then I ain't going to open your eyes. Come on, we're nearly done here.

SC: I just wanted to thank both of you for allowing us a peek into your world. It's been a real eye-opener. Do you have anything you want to say to our listeners?

AM: Don't eat yellow snow.

DD: Have a fucking Saturday.

SC: But it's Tuesday?

DD: Then have a fucking Tuesday. Slim, I ain't a calendar, I don't know what day of the week it is, my man.

Look…we spent so long, before all this happened, making things complicated, so much so that when it all got taken away, we longed for it, pined even. Life is simple, it really is. You just gotta keep close the ones you love. You just gotta stay one step ahead of those dead fucks. But…most of all…

SC: Yes?

DD: You just gotta keep livin' man. L-I-V-I-N.

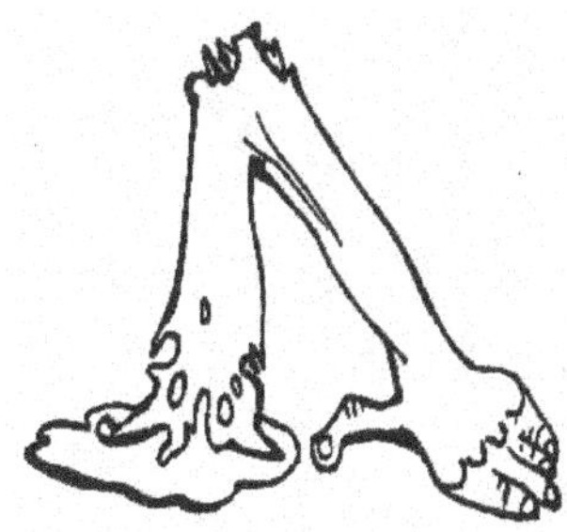

I just wanted to say a big thank you to Daryl Duncan and Adam Millard, for showing us what life is truly like in the streets and avenues of this new world. Although there are undoubtedly dark days ahead, the spirit and determination, epitomised by them and their colleagues, means that the beacon of hope shines brighter every day.

Anyway, that's all we have time for this evening. Don't forget to join me this weekend, when I bring you the radio adaptation of the eighties classic film, *Robocop*.

Following on from the success of last week's version of *The Running Man*, I cannot wait to breathe life into this timeless film.

Until then, goodnight, and remember, if you've got freedom, then you've got the skinny.

ABOUT THE AUTHOR

Duncan P. Bradshaw lit the match, and watched the fiery reflection dance across the rippling lake of petrol. How had it got to this? How many had suffered needlessly? And for what? Casting those rogue thoughts from his mind, he flicked the match, and watched on dispassionately as it tumbled through the air in slow motion. When it was on the verge of lighting up this mother**ker, he saw it flicker out.

Great.

Ah well.

Disconsolate, he deleted the words from the screen, before remembering that it was in his power to make it all come to pass. All he had to do, was write it, so he did…

Check out his website:

http://duncanpbradshaw.co.uk/

Or, even better, follow him on Facebook:

https://www.facebook.com/duncanpbradshaw/

MORE TITLES FROM THE AUTHOR

Hey there! I hope you enjoyed the array of undead stories contained within this book. If you fancy checking out the other books I've written, have a look at the following pages, hopefully there is something else I can tempt you with. There are more zombies, some sci-fi/horror, a time-spanning genre-bending EPIC and a book which will warp your mind with its utter bonkers-ness, (totally a word).

Dunk

We are all made of stars.

When an ancient Inca ritual is interrupted, it sets in motion a series of events that will echo through five hundred years of human history. Many seek to use the arcane knowledge for their own ends, from a survivor of a shipwreck, through to a suicide cult.

Yet...the most unlikeliest of them all will succeed.

"Hexagram is a visceral journey through the dark nooks and crannies of human history. Lovecraftian terror merges with blood sacrifice, suicide cults and body horror as Bradshaw weaves an intricate plot into an epic tale of apocalyptic dread."

- Rich Hawkins, author of The Last Plague trilogy

"So much more than just a horror novel, this one really makes you think. I like books that make me think, and books that present, and pull off, an original idea. This is that book and it's very much a must-read."

- Castle Macabre

PRIME DIRECTIVE

The crew of the first manned mission to Mars, are in the final days of their expedition before they head home. Shamed by a lack of discoveries and humiliated by her colleagues, geologist Dana Fischerman heads out to the Galle crater, eager to find something to make her own legacy. What she uncovers will not only threaten the safety of her colleagues, but also everyone back on Earth.

"A perfect mixture of sci-fi and horror this story plants the seed of fear in your head and makes it grow and grow until you close the book."

- Confessions of a Reviewer

"Prime Directive is filled with some fantastic comic situations and a premise that will rock your socks off."

- 2 Book Lovers Reviewers

It's the thirteenth annual Lou Gehrig awards. Four B-list celebrity virologists vie to claim the Locked In Syndrome cup and get mulched down to form their disease for mass distribution.

A disease hipster takes centre stage on a night when a blast from the past threatens to turn his ordered, pus filled life upside down. In order to blow open a deep rooted conspiracy, he must team up with a disgraced one time child star who wants another shot at the big time, and clear his sullied name.

Together, they're going to show people the real meaning of a meltdown.

"I have never read anything like this, and don't think I'll ever encounter another writer with the ability to write like this. This book is the very definition of the word 'metaphor', is very clever, and totally hilarious."

- Kayleigh Marie Edwards, author of Bitey Bachman

"Remember, you've now willingly plunged yourself into the mind of Duncan P. Bradshaw. You're completely at the mercy of his strange imagination and all the eccentric oddities that his curious mind can conjure up. Indeed, it quickly becomes apparent that the only way you'll be able to wade through the veritable quagmire of lunacy is by simply succumbing to the madness."

- DLS Reviews

Hungover, dumped and late for work.

On an ordinary day, one of these would be a bad morning, but today Jim Taylor also has to contend with the zombie apocalypse.

Follow Jim during twenty four hours of Day One, as he and his zombie obsessed brother deal with the undead, a doomsday cult and maniacs in their quest to get to their parents, win his girlfriend back and for them to instigate 'The Plan'.

Worlds will collide and fall apart in a Class Three outbreak.

"A perfect blend of humour and horror."

- Scream Magazine

"*Class Three* does a lot of interesting things that seemed quite clever. I loved how seemingly random unrelated chapters would down the line make sense and have bearing on the plot, revealing secrets that give those chapters deeper meaning."

- The Rotting Zombie

CLASS FOUR
Those Who Survive

The dead rule the world.

In the months after a deadly virus has swept across the planet, an eight year old boy and his appointed protector live from day to day. After a chance encounter they head for sanctuary. To get there, they will have to run the gauntlet of the inhabitants of this new world.

Ruled over by The Gaffer, a group of survivors holed up in a derelict factory struggle to maintain order and stability. Inside, those affected the most share their stories, hoping to come to terms with what has happened and what they've lost.

However, a clandestine operative in their midst lays the groundwork for an assault, the likes of which none of them have ever seen or could hope to prepare for.

These are the stories of those who survive.

"Action-packed, funny, and extremely brutal."

- Adam Millard, author of Vinyl Destination

"Class Four: Those Who Survive, is a total blast of a novel from beginning to end and, like its predecessor, is one of the better interpretations of the zombie apocalypse."

-Ginger Nuts of Horror

TAKE—OUT

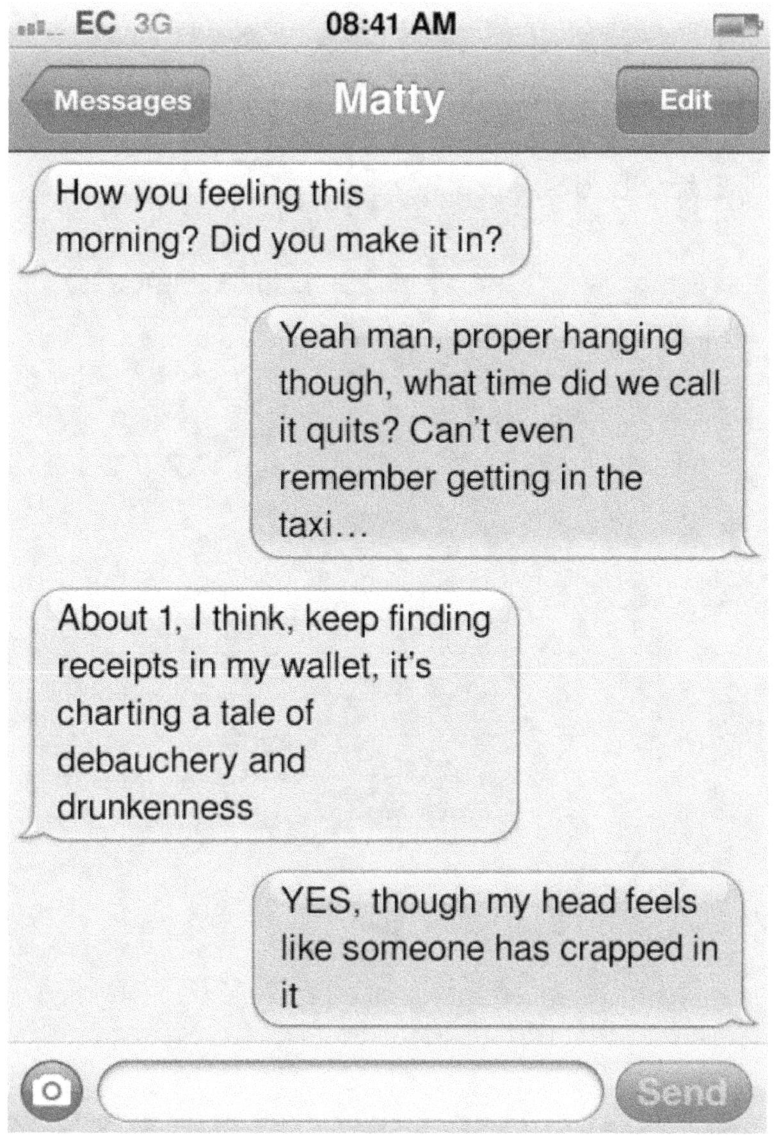
EC 3G
08:41 AM
Messages
Matty
Edit
How you feeling this morning? Did you make it in?
Yeah man, proper hanging though, what time did we call it quits? Can't even remember getting in the taxi…
About 1, I think, keep finding receipts in my wallet, it's charting a tale of debauchery and drunkenness
YES, though my head feels like someone has crapped in it
Send

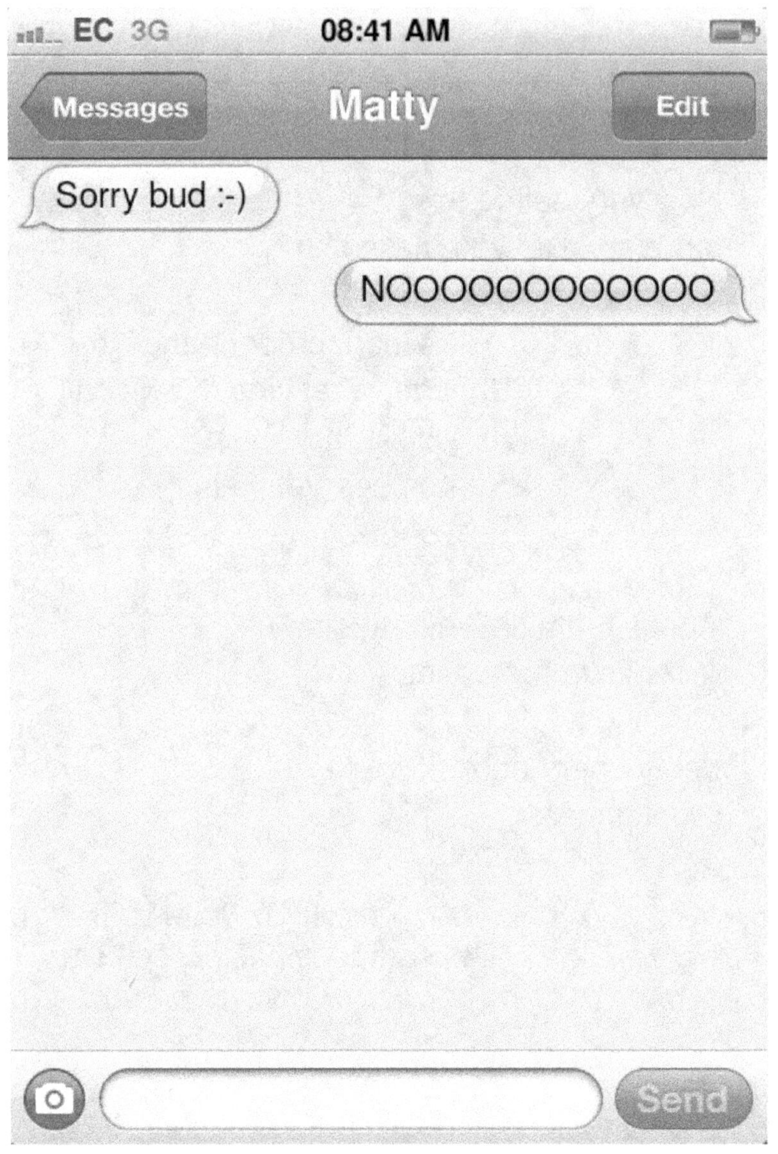
EC 3G
08:41 AM
Messages
Matty
Edit
Sorry bud :-)
NOOOOOOOOOOOO
Send

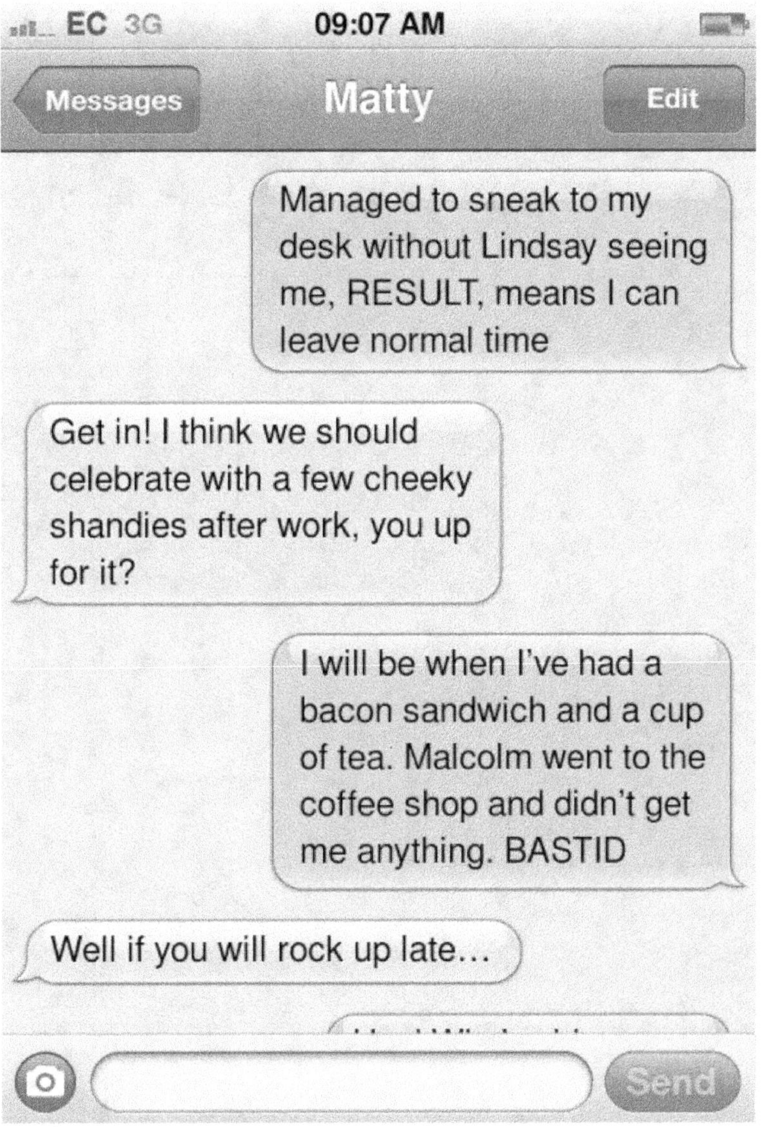
EC 3G
09:07 AM
Messages
Matty
Edit
Managed to sneak to my desk without Lindsay seeing me, RESULT, means I can leave normal time
Get in! I think we should celebrate with a few cheeky shandies after work, you up for it?
I will be when I've had a bacon sandwich and a cup of tea. Malcolm went to the coffee shop and didn't get me anything. BASTID
Well if you will rock up late…
Send

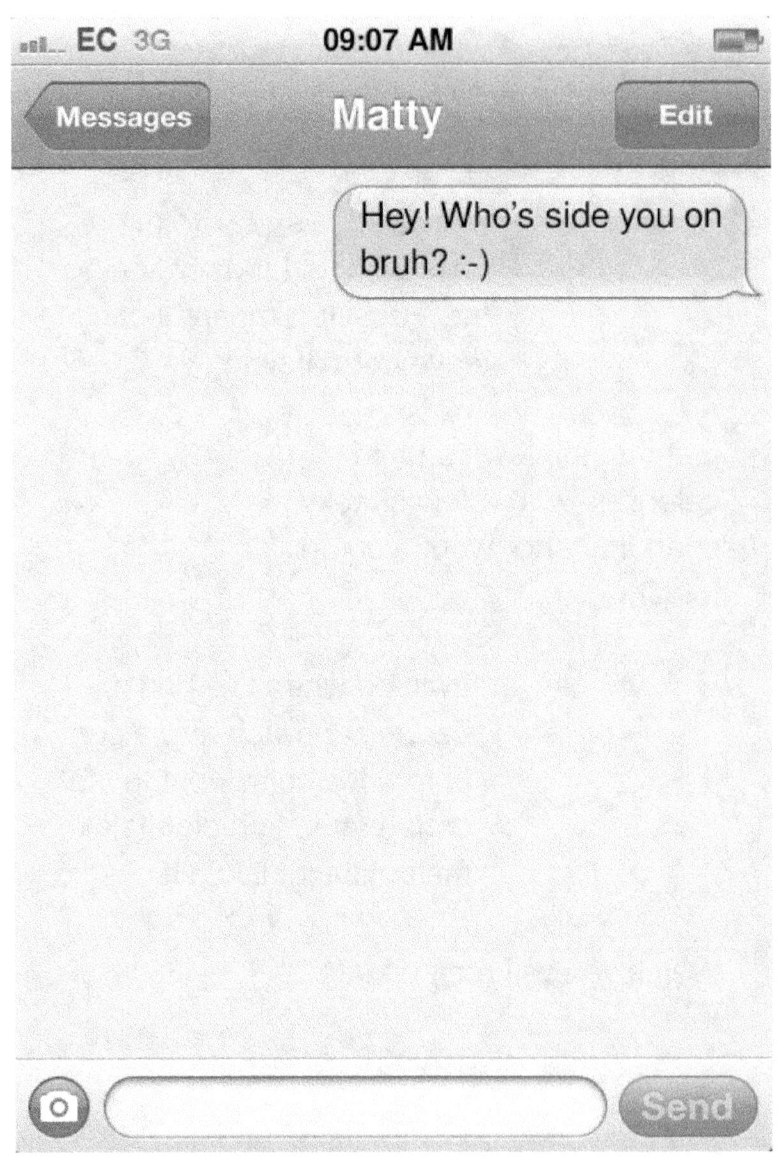
EC 3G
09:07 AM
Messages
Matty
Edit
Hey! Who's side you on bruh? :-)
Send

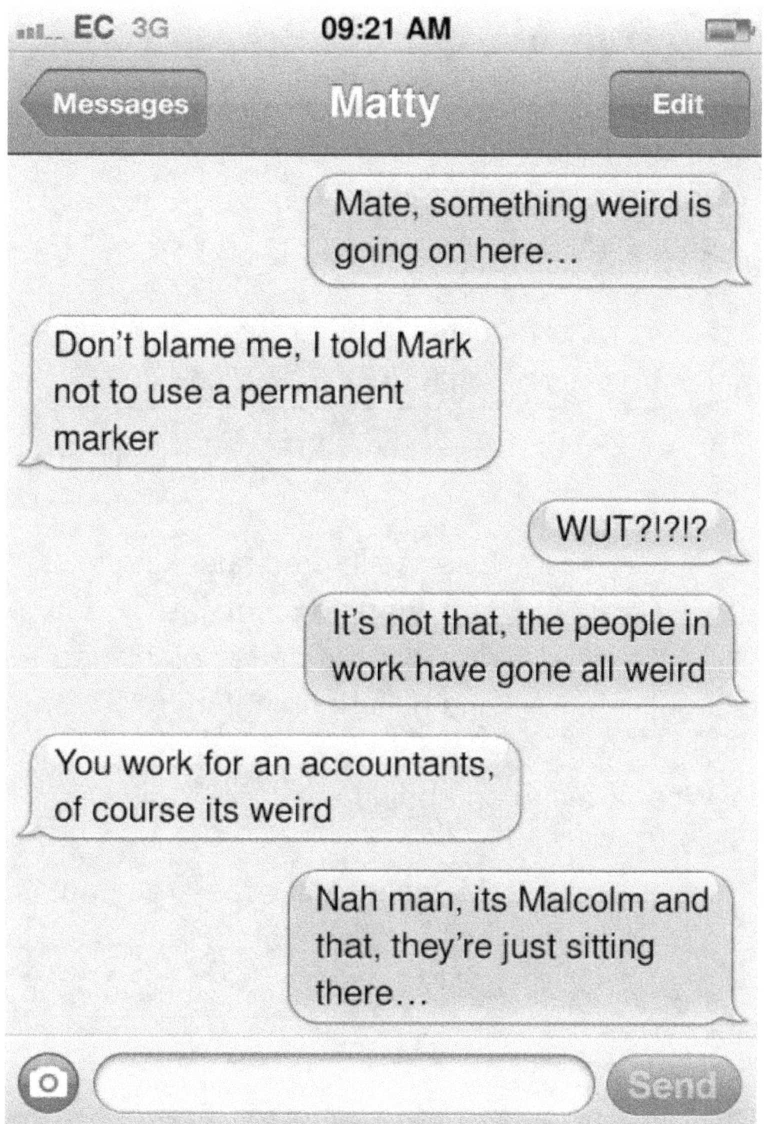
EC 3G
09:21 AM
Messages
Matty
Edit
Mate, something weird is going on here…
Don't blame me, I told Mark not to use a permanent marker
WUT?!?!?
It's not that, the people in work have gone all weird
You work for an accountants, of course its weird
Nah man, its Malcolm and that, they're just sitting there…
Send

EC 3G
09:21 AM
Messages
Matty
Edit
Taking a leaf out of your book then? :-D
This is different man, this is mad AF
I can't wake him!
Like at all, tried speaking to him, slapping him, jus dropped his coffee on his leg and he's done nuffin
What are you on about?
Malcolm! His eyes are open, but he's not doing ANYTHING
Send

EC 3G
09:21 AM
Messages
Matty
Edit
Shit, shit, shit, there are loads of them like this…most of the team have gone weird man, what do I do?
Erm…have you seen the news?
Mate, I'm more worried about my FUBAR workmates right now
DOOD, YOUR OFFICE IS ON THE NEWS
LIKE NOW!!!!!
Dude?
Send

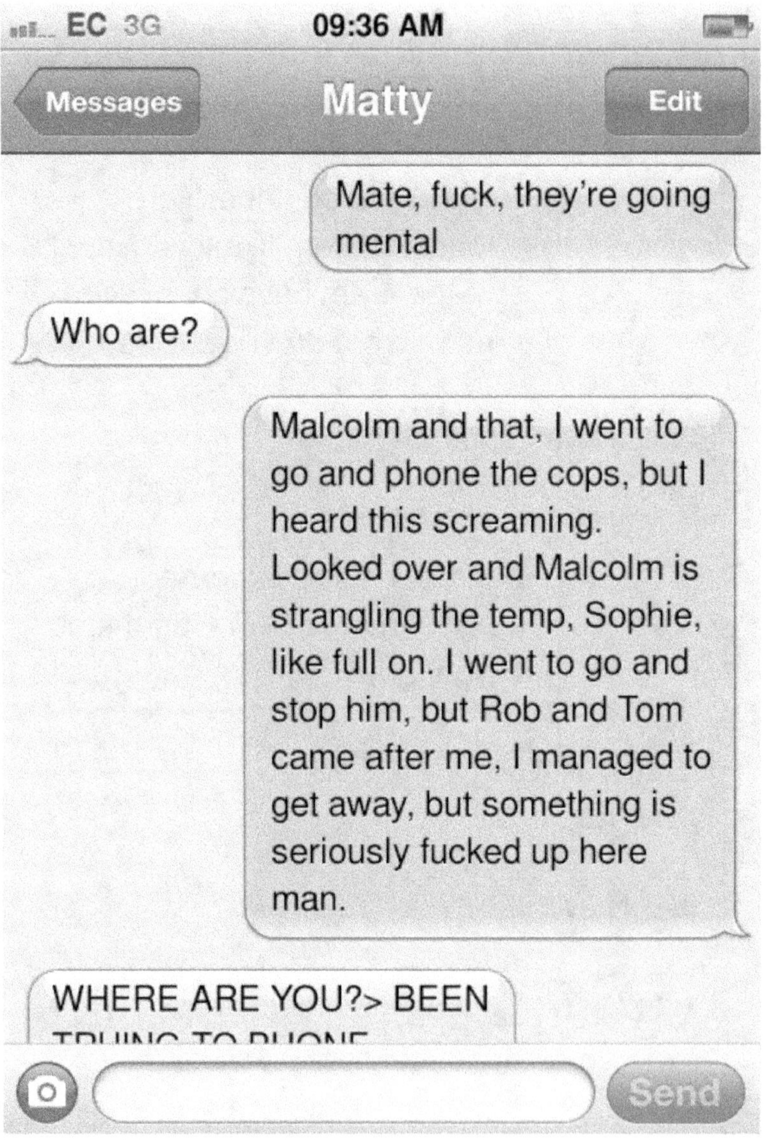
EC 3G
09:36 AM
Messages
Matty
Edit
Mate, fuck, they're going mental
Who are?
Malcolm and that, I went to go and phone the cops, but I heard this screaming. Looked over and Malcolm is strangling the temp, Sophie, like full on. I went to go and stop him, but Rob and Tom came after me, I managed to get away, but something is seriously fucked up here man.
WHERE ARE YOU?> BEEN
Send

EC 3G
09:36 AM
Messages
Matty
Edit
WHERE ARE YOU?> BEEN TRUING TO PHONE
On silent. Hiding. Phone the cops, there's mne and som others, we're in the second floor meeting room,
South side, facing thr stret, HURRRY UP
Mate, the news is saying that there are people falling out of windows at your place?!??! WHT'S GOING ON?????!?
Mate?
Send

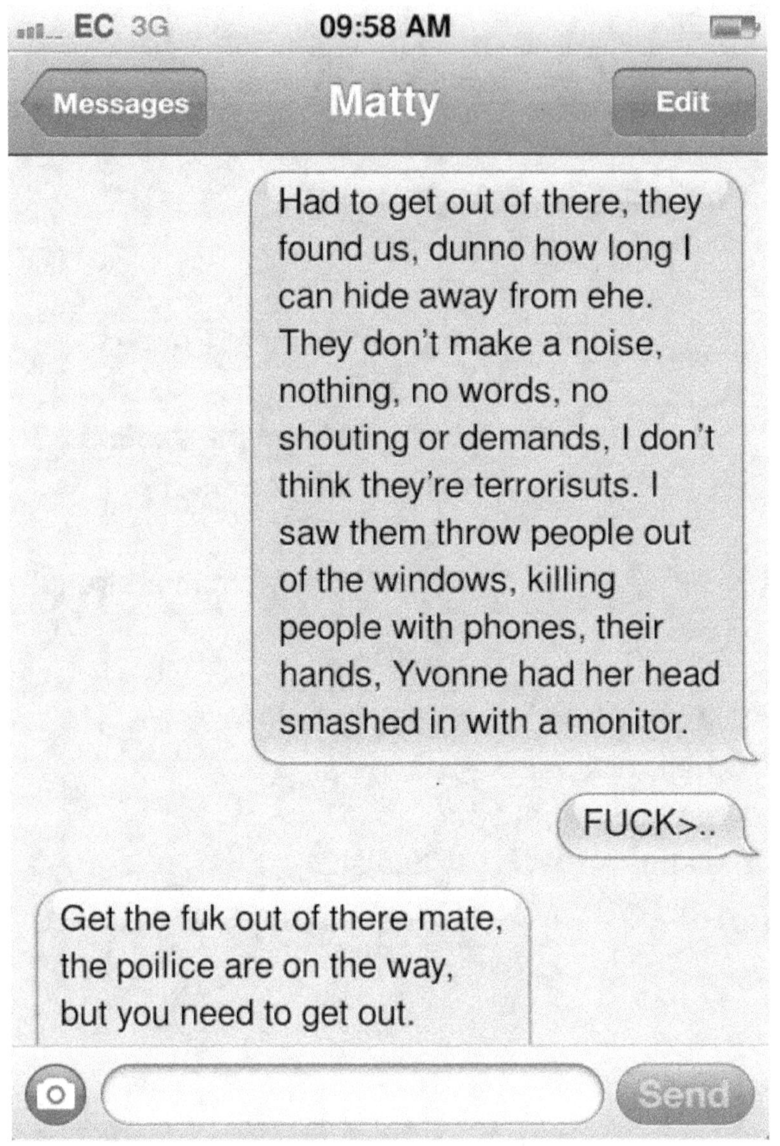

EC 3G
09:58 AM
Messages
Matty
Edit
Had to get out of there, they found us, dunno how long I can hide away from ehe. They don't make a noise, nothing, no words, no shouting or demands, I don't think they're terrorisuts. I saw them throw people out of the windows, killing people with phones, their hands, Yvonne had her head smashed in with a monitor.
FUCK>..
Get the fuk out of there mate, the poilice are on the way, but you need to get out.
Send